Ab

Wesley Burrowes [...] [...] Down, in 1930. [...] University Belfas [...] he began writing for the theatre, winning the Irish Life Drama Award in two successive years. Recruited by RTÉ, he was principal writer of the long-running drama serial *Bracken*, from which he created the even-longer running *Glenroe*. On three occasions, he won the Jacobs (National Television) Award and, in 1992, a Telecom National Entertainment Award.

In more recent years, he has been writing film scripts, including *Circle of Deceit* (1993), *Rat* (1999) and *Mystics*, due for release in 2002.

He has one son, Kim, and one daughter, Ciara, and lives in Bray, County Wicklow with his wife, Helena.

Downhill Farm

The Final Episode

Wesley Burrowes

**TOWN
HOUSE**
DUBLIN

First published in 2002 by

TownHouse and CountryHouse Ltd

Trinity House

Charleston Road

Ranelagh

Dublin 6

Ireland

1 2 3 4 5 6 7 8 9 10

A CIP catalogue record for this book is available from the British Library.

ISBN: 1-86059-168-X

Cover design by Splash, London

Typeset by Typeform Ltd, Dublin

Printed by Bookmarque, London

To Helena

Glossary

O.S.	offscreen
POV	point of view
a beat	a short pause
INT	interior
EXT	exterior
sparks	electricians
chippies	carpenters

1

In the wide front yard of Downhill Farm in County Wexford, the Days were preparing to leave home.

By the door of the Georgian farmhouse, Dermot Day was tying down the back gate of the Jeep, packed tight with boxes, suitcases and tea-chests.

A row of stone outhouses ran the length of the yard. The one at the end had curtained windows and a red creeper, and in its doorway the two old farm workers, Liam and Eric, stood watching. They had lived here all their lives, long before Dermot's time. Away to the south, at the bottom of the steep hill that gave the farm its name, ran the river where they had fished since they were boys. There was even a sunset, the last rays shining through a row of poplars, lighting the tall windows of the house. If you saw it as a painting on a gallery wall, you would say it was too much and pass on.

Across the yard, outside the big, red barn, Dermot's younger brothers, Peter and Luke, finished bolting up the tailgate of the truck carrying the furniture, checked the tyres and walked across to join him.

'All set?' he asked.

They nodded. What was there to say?

'Better get the girls.'

As Luke and Peter walked into the house, Dermot bent to tighten the last knot, and heard a voice behind him.

'That'll do her.'

As he turned, Liam came past him, testing the ropes for tightness, shaking his head.

Dermot smiled. He had learned not to expect praise from either of them.

'Sorry it had to end this way, lads.'

Liam gave a toss of the head.

'Sure what harm? I was thinkin' of takin' early retirement anyway. The redundancy package.'

Dermot grinned and shook Eric's hand.

'You'll look after him, Eric?'

Eric never smiled. 'Isn't it a pity they closed the workhouse?' he said.

'Who needs it?' said Dermot. 'Your home's safe.'

'Don't know about that,' said Liam. 'Once you're gone they could knock the whole lot. Put up a nightclub.'

Dermot shook his head. 'It's in the contract. Yours for life.'

'Jaze, now, Dermot,' said Eric. 'No man could have done more.'

Dermot looked startled. The first compliment he had ever heard from Eric.

And now Liam was joining in. 'I remember the day you came first, a child in arms…'

'I was twenty-three.'

Liam ignored him.

'The house was in rack and ruin. And the land was nothin' only scrub and stones and bracken.'

'And the gorse bushes,' said Eric. ''Twas a miracle you ever got it cleared.'

'Well, I had the best of help,' started Dermot.

But for Liam, the soft talk was over, the subject closed.

'Where is it again you're going?' he asked.

'Scotland. Argyllshire.'

Eric repeated the name softly.

'Were you ever in Scotland, Liam?' he asked.

'Never was.' Liam spoke as if he'd been accused.

'I hear it's not half settled.'

'Where we're going,' said Dermot, 'it's a lot like Wexford. The house is falling down, but the land's good.'

As he spoke, Peter and Luke came from the house with the girls. First Dermot's young wife, Lisa, little Stephen in her arms, then his sisters, Maire and Aisling.

Aisling, in tears, came straight to Liam and hugged him, a rare experience for him, and not one he enjoyed.

'Oh, Liam!'

She moved from Liam to Eric, kissing his cheek.

'Eric, what'll we do without you?'

Maire and Lisa followed, a little more restrained.

'We'll write,' said Lisa.

'And we'll come back and see you,' sobbed Aisling.

'And bring you both a kilt.' Maire, the eldest, trying to lighten things.

Peter glanced up at the sky.

'Time we were gone,' he said. 'If we want the last of the light.'

Luke and Peter moved to the truck. Dermot opened the doors of the Jeep for the girls and climbed in himself.

Liam and Eric stood back.

'What way are ye going?'

'N11 to Dublin, straight to the North on the M1, then the ferry from Larne. It's a fine evening. Should be a good crossing.'

He could think of nothing more. He started the engine, then turned his head to take a last look at the house. As the Jeep moved slowly off, the girls made little miniature waves with their fingers and shaped their lips into goodbyes. First the Jeep, then the truck, moved out of the yard and down the narrow byroad, past the wooden shingle that said 'Downhill Farm'. As they moved round the corner and out of sight, the last of the sun dipped down below the rim of the Blackstairs Mountains.

For a few seconds, the yard was silent. Then a voice, from a source not yet seen, spoke quietly.

'Hold it and… cut!'

Then he appeared around the gable end of the farmhouse. Tall, thin, forty, holding a clipboard, Lance the director strode into the picture, calling to an army of technicians who appeared from nowhere to converge in the yard.

'Great work everybody, thank you all. Check it, Willie.'

The cameraman was already playing it back. The floor manager, the sound men, sparks and chippies, riggers and runners, all talking at once. From the house came the PA and the stage manager, with large trays of champagne and glasses. And over it all the voice of Lance telling everyone how bloody marvellous they all were.

Willie the cameraman finished his check and came to join them.

'All clear, Lance,' he said, and a cheer went up.

'Thank Christ,' said Lance, as he looked up at a sky growing darker by the second.

'We'd have been back tomorrow.'

Cheers went up as Liam and Eric emerged from the house, bowing gravely in acknowledgement. There was a not-too-subtle change in their demeanour. Liam was now wearing a silk scarf, Eric smoking a cigar. They accepted their champagne in the manner of people who drank nothing else.

Lance put an arm round the neck of each and hugged them, spilling their drinks.

'Thanks, lads,' he said, his Cork accent filled with sincerity. 'Ye never lost it.'

Liam took the glass from his lips. 'Good take, was it?'

'Bloody miraculous.'

Lance glanced over at the door of the house, where another crew appeared to be setting up, but he passed no remarks.

'Rather strange, though,' said Eric. 'Our Mr O'Hara.'

'You're just discovering that, are you?'

'Oh, I have no illusions. He's been many things down the years, but to be late on set, today of all days. Did he say why?'

Lance nodded towards the gate. 'Why don't you ask him?'

As the Jeep and the truck drove back into the yard, Lance began the applause, and the rest of the crew and cast joined in. The actors jumped down, Maire and Aisling, Lisa and little Stephen, Peter and Luke, and there was an orgy of embracing, even tears. Just one actor stayed by the Jeep. Conor O'Hara, who played the role of Dermot Day.

Lance held his arms wide and the cast walked one by one into his embrace. He kissed them all, men, women and children, with equal fervour, then looked over at Conor, who stood, oblivious of the rest, staring around at all the familiar sights, as if trying to fix them in his memory.

Lance sighed, muttered a few 'Excuse mes' and walked over to join him. Conor stood motionless, staring at the sky. Lance hesitated before deciding to break the moment.

'Well, Conor. End of an era.'

Conor gave a startled look, as if seeing him for the first time.

'How does it feel?'

Conor shook his head.

'Impossible to say. It's like a dream, a journey into another place, another time. Leaving behind everything I know… every tree, every leaf.'

He began walking slowly towards the house. Lance took a deep breath and followed.

The cast and crew, talking all at once, went quiet as Conor passed, then broke into a ripple of applause. Conor gave them a small inclination of the head.

'Bless you all,' he said.

Eric and Liam exchanged a jaundiced look and reached for another glass.

As Conor and Lance approached the farmhouse door, the cameraman and soundman who had set up there moved back respectfully. An outsider might have thought that Conor had not noticed them but, as Lance was all too aware, Conor always knew where the camera was.

'This was real, you see,' said Conor, running his hand along the smooth-worn top of the half-door. 'Look. You see the stain?'

Lance nodded.

'Where Aisling tried to climb over and fell on her nose, remember?

'Bled for hours.'

As he turned away, someone behind the curtain of the ground-floor window, someone in a suit, ducked out of sight. Conor went on.

'But it's not real any more… not the reality I knew. Someone will move in here. Paint this over.'

Across the yard, riggers and stage hands were carrying painted flats from the barn and loading them into a truck. Conor watched them.

'After all these years, the final wrap.'

No-one spoke for a moment. Then, from the door of the house, a new voice.

'Not quite,' it said. 'There's one more scene.'

Conor whipped round. The man who had spoken stood smiling, holding a microphone in one hand, a bright-red book in the other. For a moment, Conor was taken unawares.

'Michael!' he said, with the instant familiarity always accorded to the very famous.

The cast and crew, all of them privy to what was happening, pressed forward, giggling like children. Michael turned to the camera and spoke.

'Tonight, as you see, we are down on the farm. Not just any old farm, but one I think we've all come to know intimately in the last fifteen years. We've come here today to watch the final filming of the final scene of the greatly loved drama serial, *The Days of Downhill Farm*…'

He turned to Conor and the camera pulled back for the two-shot.

'... and to say to *you*, Conor O'Hara, alias Dermot Day, Head of the Family, Star of the Show, tonight – *This... is Your Life.'*

Instinctively, on seeing him, Conor had rehearsed his reaction. Modest, tongue-tied. And, as always, beautifully played. A look round at the cast, a shake of the head, a whisper. 'I don't believe it.'

Three long limousines had crept quietly through the gate and, as he was led to the first of them, still shaking his head, the camera swung to show the cast and crew as they followed, clapping and giggling.

Eric and Liam were last to move. Eric looked weary.

'Come on, old chap,' said Liam. 'The show must go on.'

'Must it?' said Eric.

Then, knowing their duty and, more importantly, knowing their place, they followed.

* * *

Conor's parents had both been teachers. His father had taught history, his mother English. So it seemed natural, when his schooldays ended, that he, too, should become a teacher. He had been a fair student at school, where he found he could get out of playing rugby by volunteering for the school play, which was always Shakespeare. He made his debut as Ursula, a rather unimportant lady-in-waiting in *Much Ado About Nothing*, and went on to greater success as Lady Macbeth. The school magazine said that: 'CJ O'Hara (Form IVA) was a splendidly chilling Lady Macbeth.' He still kept the clipping.

The next year, he was to play Mistress Quickly in *Henry IV Part 1*, but his voice broke and he played Prince Hal. A year later, he had his final triumph as *Othello*.

After a year of increasing boredom as a teacher, and missing the escape of the stage, he decided to join the Abbey School of Acting and began to spend all his free time there. He had never much enjoyed the chat in the staff common room, but here, sharing his enthusiasms with kindred spirits, he found a new life. And it helped that he had grown handsome. He had found a very small flat close to the Grand Canal where the rising actresses of the Abbey School were only too pleased to come back and talk Strindberg far into the night.

As part of the training, the students were doing walk-ons in the main theatre. He was an Aran fisherman in *Riders to the Sea* and an English Tommy in *The Plough and the Stars*. He also understudied. And when the actor playing Shawn Keogh in *The Playboy of the Western World* reported in drunk, he took over. He played the part for just two nights, but he made an impression. There was even a line, in *The Irish Times* 'Front Row' column, about an exciting new talent. An important exposure.

And so, when the decision was made to revive Lennox Robinson's *The Whiteheaded Boy* the following season, and Conor was asked to play him, there was no hesitation.

Now twenty-four, and against his parents' advice, he gave up the steady job at St Felix's National School and became an actor. *The Whiteheaded Boy* had a record run and Conor, from nowhere, had arrived.

When the national television station decided on a new long-running drama serial about a young man, newly bereaved, taking over the family farm in Wexford and at the same time bringing up a family of young siblings, the only name considered was Conor O'Hara. He was accustomed now to being a public figure, and had learned how to deal with it. And when they asked him to what he attributed his success, he would shake his head, look at the floor and say modestly that he had been lucky.

* * *

The television theatre was full to bursting. Watching at home, you'd have said seven or eight hundred, but in fact just a hundred and eighty, half in new outfits, the rest studiously casual. The first few rows would be friends and families of cast and crew. Further back the more obscure connections. Someone who lived next door to someone who worked for the sponsors, someone whose son was walking out with someone from make-up, someone who won the tickets in a pub quiz.

Another fifty-odd sat on banks of seats on either side of the stage. Important people, but not the household names who would come on later, making entrances. The seats on stage left were already filled with dignitaries, in decreasing order of importance from front to back. In front, controllers of programmes, heads of drama, heads of development, heads of drama development, heads of development (drama). In the midst of the heads sat Tony, producer of *The Days of Downhill Farm* and its senior director, Lance. Behind them sat other directors and high-ranking techies, designers, directors of photography and film editors. Behind those, assistant directors, sound engineers, vision mixers, wardrobe and make-up. Behind those, in the back row, sat the writers, blinking, unaccustomed to the light.

On stage right, the front row was empty, and in the rows behind sat the actors from *The Days*, past and present, or at least all those who would not be called on to make an individual entrance, in praise of the main man, Conor. In the audience, some played the game of pointing at the actors and trying to remember the roles they had played, who had married whom; with whom, in fact or fiction, they had been unfaithful, when they had died or gone to Peru. Others peered at the TV monitor on stage, watching mute scenes from the last fifteen years of *The Days*, placing them in time, agreeing and disagreeing over what happened next.

Each had been given, on the way in, a souvenir programme of the evening. On the front, a brief history of each of the Days since they first appeared on the nation's screens fifteen years ago. And on the back, a list of those cast members who would appear tonight. There would be much autographing before the night was done.

Dermot Day	Conor O'Hara
Tara Day	Linda Lee
Lisa Day	Samantha Black
Maire Day	Eve Staunton
Peter Day	Paul Rogers
Luke Day	Rory Bell
Aisling Day	Roisín Molloy
Liam O'Kelly	Frank Dooley
Eric Blair	TP Muldowney
Sir Myles Tregorran	Godfrey Standish
Lady Daphne Tregorran	Sylvana O'Brien
Stephen Day	Mark Staunton

Two cameramen were in position on stage, one more in the auditorium facing the audience, another in the aisles. Sound operators checked the mikes on stage, while others moved about the auditorium waving their furry booms. Researchers, girls with cans and clipboards, came back and forth from backstage with messages.

Dick, the floor manager, who, in the tradition of floor managers, swore a lot, finished checking the glasses of water, cupped a hand to his ear, listened a moment, then walked to the edge of the stage and signalled for silence.

As he spoke, the lights dimmed in the auditorium.

'I just got word that Michael – and tonight's star guest – are on their way. In less than two minutes we'll be on the air, and I want you to remember that your contribution to the show is vital. So will you all get ready, put your hands together and when I give the signal, give it all you've got.'

A glance behind.

'All right, we're on the countdown. Let's make this a show to remember.'

The sig music began and Dick darted to the side of the stage, holding up his hands, his arms bent at the elbows, like a stick-up victim. The music swelled in volume, Dick's hands shot upward, the audience clapped and cheered and Conor appeared at the back of the stage, the great Michael a step behind.

For a moment, Conor stood and stared about, overcome. Then Michael took his elbow and guided him downstage, as the audience responded to Dick's urging with greater and greater applause. On stage, the distinguished guests were also on their feet, paying their tribute. Conor bowed to them, pointing to one, then another, feigning delight and surprise to see them there. Then, as he reached his mike, he walked past it and held out his hands to his audience, smiling, baffled by it all. Michael let it go for a moment, then stepped forward and brought Conor back to his mark. Out of vision, Dick was

14

signalling for the applause to fade, pressing his palms on the lid of an imaginary suitcase.

The camera zoomed slowly in on Michael as he turned to Conor and the show began.

'Tonight, Conor O'Hara, actor, better known to us all as Dermot Day, fruit-farmer, *This is Your Life*. And perhaps, for the benefit of those who have been asleep or abroad for a very long time, let me fill in a little of your background.

'We first met Dermot more than fifteen years ago, when his own parents, still in their prime, died in a plane crash, leaving Dermot, a lad of twenty-three, to bring up a brood of younger brothers and sisters. For those fifteen years we've been watching all of them growing up on Downhill Farm in County Wexford.

'And here they are. Maire... Peter... Luke... Aisling.'

His voice rose to compete with the applause which greeted the four handsome young people who came on in quick succession as their names were called.

'The Days of Downhill Farm,' he finished, and they stood milking it for a moment, until Dick persuaded the audience to cool it and they took their seats in the front row.

'And finally,' said Michael, 'Dermot's lovely young wife, Lisa, and the youngest Day of all – Stephen!'

Lisa came on, smiling and waving, carrying the toddler Stephen. Conor kissed both and ushered them to the seats reserved for them, beside him. Michael, his red book open at page one, stood over them. All of them were instantly recognisable, like old friends, but there was a poise, a confidence, a knowledge of how to sit, how to look, how to behave, that would have seemed out of place in the characters they played.

And they seemed determined to demonstrate those differences, to show perhaps how good those performances were, the art of artlessness. Only one, Conor himself, came over exactly as the character he played.

'Now, Lisa,' Michael began.

'It's Sam,' she interrupted. She gave a dazzling smile. The kind of smile that Lisa Day would never have managed.

'Ah, yes, of course. Hard to think of you as anything but Lisa. But tell me, Sam. Is it true that you prefer older men?'

'Within reason,' she said.

The audience smiled happily, and Conor smiled with them, showing what a good sport he was.

'And what's it like to have a husband that half the women in the country lust after?'

'Well, I only have him in make-believe, haven't I?'

'But do people…' Michael pretended to search for words. '… ask you things?'

Sam played along.

'What kind of things?'

'Well… intimate things, if you follow me?'

'You mean, like… what's he like in bed?'

The audience giggled. Conor smiled ruefully.

'They do, honestly,' Sam went on. 'In fact, I've been asked far worse.'

'Yes, yes, I think we've got the idea,' said Michael, hastily. 'But you don't find it upsetting?'

'No, no, I rather enjoy it. My boyfriend's not so keen.'

Conor sat looking up at the lights.

'And what about *you*, Conor? You don't mind if I call you Conor?'

'Well, it's my name.'

'Yes, but, for the entire country, and perhaps a few other countries where the Days are known, you are Dermot Day. Don't you ever get tired of people pointing at you and calling your name?'

Conor considered a moment.

'I find people very kind as a rule. Very polite.' On the onstage monitor, he was in close-up. 'And if they come and talk to you as if they've known you for years, well, that's a compliment isn't it? Not just to *me* but to the show. All of us.'

He spread his arms, to include all the others who sat alongside and behind. 'It's a privilege. One I'd never take for granted.'

But as he spoke, he was remembering a day, three years ago, a day in summer. Nothing out of the ordinary had happened, and yet, looking back, it was the day it all began to go wrong…

Conor stepped out of the lift, nodded to the man on the desk and walked across the terrazzo floor to the door, enjoying the castanet click of his heeltaps. He had moved into his apartment on Dublin's south quays five years ago and, though he seemed quite at ease with its opulence, he was, in truth, still getting used to it. He shouldered his way through the glass doors, turned up his collar, lowered his head and set off down the quay to his car park. He had learned the trick of walking with his head lowered while remaining aware of what lay ahead. Two young women were coming to meet him, giggling and whispering. There was no way around. He pulled up as if spotting them late and begged their pardon. They smiled foolishly at him.

'Excuse us, Mr Day,' said one.

Her friend was quick to correct her. 'O'Hara,' she whispered.

'Mr O'Hara, sorry,' said the first one. 'I was wonderin' – could I have your autograph?'

She had her shorthand notebook out and Conor found himself wondering if people still did shorthand.

'I'm sorry to bother you,' she said.

'No bother at all,' said Conor, taking the book. 'What name?'

'Carmel.'

As he began to write, the friend, anxious to be part of it all, told him that they all loved the programme.

'You're very kind,' he said, smiling, nodding and moving modestly on.

'Gizza look?' said the friend, taking the notebook and reading aloud.

'To the lovely Carmel… from Conor O'Hara.'

The lovely Carmel turned to watch him go.

'Isn't he gorgeous?' she whispered.

Conor kept going. On the river side of the road, a dozen girls in school uniforms stood waiting to cross, talking like mynah birds. Instinctively, Conor speeded up, turning his head towards the shop windows. Too late.

'Hey, would you look who it is?'

'Who?'

He kept going.

'Him off the telly. Come on!'

He had a decent start, and as he heard them starting to cross, he took a fast left turn into a narrow street. Behind him, the voices were calling.

'Dermot! Hey, Dermot, wait for *us*!'

Just ahead of him, he saw a couple coming from a doorway. As they moved away Conor stepped smartly inside and found an inner glass door bearing the words 'Café Vangelis', in Aegean blue. Below, in black and white, a card said 'Open'.

He pushed the door, went inside, grabbed a chair and sat facing the wall.

People sitting at tables and three girls who seemed to be waitresses looked at him in surprise, but he saw none of them. From outside came the squeals of the chasing pack of schoolgirls but, in a moment, they were past and the youngest of the three waitresses came over to him. It was plain, from her look of contained excitement, that she had recognised him.

'Were they after you?'

'I'm afraid so.'

'I think the coast is clear.'

He looked cautiously over his shoulder at the window, then turned his chair and smiled up at her.

'What can I get you?'

'Oh, just a coffee I think. Espresso.'

'We're good at that.' She grinned and went off to the serving hatch.

'One espresso,' she called.

'Comin' up,' said a voice from inside and, as the girl moved away from the hatch, Conor saw a little dark woman shifting pots, in the manner of someone well used to it. As she moved out of sight, he heard her whistling 'Summertime', which struck him as strange. Not many women whistled.

He opened his *Irish Times* and, pretending to read, took a look around the Café Vangelis. It was an intimate room, eight or nine small tables with blue-checked cloths.

On the walls were prints of Greek islands, white churches with little bell towers, blinding white between the electric blues of sea and sky. Caïques with Greek names: *Eleni*, *Angelikki*, fishermen with moustaches. Old men in pantaloons, perched side-saddle on donkeys. More old men outside a Kafeneion, playing Tavli.

Only two of the tables were occupied. At one, a young couple gazed at each other over a bowl of salad. At the other, three middle-aged ladies were discussing Conor furtively, the two dark ones trying to press the blondey one into action.

'Go on, he won't eat you.'

And, eventually, the blondey one took her menu card, got up and came over to him.

'Mr O'Hara?'

Conor lowered his paper, looked into her eyes.

'I'm sorry for disturbing you, but… well, we all feel we know you.'

'You're very kind,' said Conor.

She put the menu before him. 'I wondered if you could sign this?'

'Of course.'

'It's for me daughter. Sharon.'

As he wrote, with the old-fashioned fountain pen he kept specially, the waitress put the little cup of espresso on the table beside him and slipped away. The blondey one gave a little proud smile to her friends. With a small flourish, Conor finished writing.

'Thank you, you're very good.'

'A pleasure,' said Conor, and sipped his coffee.

Back at their table, the two dark ladies peered at the menu. The blondey one read it out in a whisper.

'To the lovely Sharon… from Conor O'Hara.'

She gave a small contented smile.

'He's exactly the same as he is in reality,' she added, mysteriously.

'Is the coffee all right?' said the little waitress.

'Perfect,' said Conor.

She lowered her voice. 'I'm sorry if that lady was botherin' you.'

'No, no, I didn't mind in the least,' said Conor.

He drained the tiny cup and put his hand in his pocket.

'Ah, no, that's from me.'

'Oh, how very kind,' he said.

She smiled, embarrassed.

'What's your name?'

'Rose.'

'Well, thank you, Rose.'

'It's really nice to have you in here.'

'I'll be back, I promise.'

He stood, gave a little bow and walked to the door, where he turned and smiled.

Rose and the three ladies smiled back. Behind them, through the hatch, Conor had a glimpse of the little dark woman. She smiled at him absently, as she would smile at any other customer, and went on whistling 'Summertime'.

2

'But of course, Sam,' said Michael, you weren't the *first* Mrs Day, were you?'

The cameras were still on Sam or, as she was better known, the lovely Lisa Day.

Sam shook her head, her eyebrows arched widely. Michael turned to the audience.

'Twelve years ago, Dermot decided he needed someone to er… help with the chores, and married Tara. You remember Tara?'

The audience nodded and mumbled, smiling foolishly.

'They were together for less than two years, but we thought, on this special occasion, we might reunite them. So please welcome the lovely… Linda Lee!'

Dick leapt into action and the audience responded with loud applause as an elegant woman, about Conor's age, came on from behind and walked downstage, smiling. Her old colleagues onstage rose to welcome her, and Conor, plainly delighted, came to meet and embrace

23

her. And as the applause faded, the two stood hand-in-hand.

'What a wonderful introduction,' said Linda.

'Not so much an introduction,' said Michael, 'as a resurrection.'

A few giggles came from the audience, and Dick whipped it up as best he could.

'As I recall,' said Michael, 'you had a rather spectacular death. But we'll talk later about your final exit. Tell us now about your entrance. How did it all start for you?'

'Gosh,' said Linda. 'It's all so long ago.'

She had been asked that question, or one like it, a hundred times before, but it always seemed to take her by surprise. And yet she remembered every moment...

Her mother had been an actress. Not a very successful one, but she was determined that her daughter would succeed where she had failed. So little Linda had been taught elocution, tap-dancing, ballet, piano and harp, and was enrolled in acting school from the age of eight. She grew up in an all-singing, all-dancing world and though her opinion was not asked, she never liked it much. She would have much preferred to spend Christmas at home, opening her presents, rather than hoofing on a pantomime stage dressed as an elf.

When she was eighteen, she finally persuaded her mother, who had always meant well, that 'hi-diddley-dee, an actor's life for me' was not actually the career choice she had in mind. She had met a boy called Freddy, six years older than she was, who wanted to marry her. He was an economics graduate working in his father's bank. Her mother, who had never met anyone who owned a bank, agreed not to stand in Linda's way, but asked her, as a special favour, if she would stay on in the Abbey School of Acting, where she had just enrolled.

Linda was happy to do that. It was still acting, but it was grown-up acting.

It was almost a year later that a wonderful new man joined the school. His name was Conor O'Hara and she loved him from the first moment. And although several of the other girls seemed to have the same ideas, she knew that he liked her best. And in fact he told her so, in the long enchanted evenings and Arabian nights they spent together in his flat by the canal. But it was all hopeless. The plans for her marriage to Freddy were irreversibly made, the house bought and furnished, the marquee ready in his father's garden, the gift list in Brown Thomas. So she had married Freddy and gone on honeymoon to Mustique and come back to Killiney and settled down.

Conor phoned her from time to time, and once or twice they met, unarranged, and had a coffee. She read about him in the papers of course and went three times to see him in *The Whiteheaded Boy*. And when *The Days of Downhill Farm* began on television, she watched every moment, and the repeats. Then one day, out of the blue, he phoned her to ask if she would be interested in auditioning for the part of his new wife. He couldn't promise anything but he had some influence. It was the best moment of her life.

To be married to him, even in make-believe…

She looked up to see Michael looking down at her.

'It's not so long ago,' he was saying. 'Just twelve years. But how did you come to get the part? I mean, you weren't exactly a household name, were you?'

'No,' Linda agreed. 'I'd done a little theatre work when I was younger, but I gave that up when I got married.'

'To Freddy,' said Michael, by way of a prompt.

'Yes,' she said, and smiled down at the audience, where Camera 3 was already in position, giving the viewers a picture of a smiling, fleshy man in a fawn suit, his hair a curious shade of dark mahogany.

'But you see, Freddy was doing more and more travelling for his business and I was left a good deal on my own, so I started auditioning again. And when I was offered Tara, well, I jumped at the chance.'

'And we're all delighted you did. Let's see you as you were in those early days, at the Wexford Strawberry Fair!'

He swung his arm around to the onstage monitor, as the pictures came up.

The playback was of a day ten years ago, but Conor, who was good on lines, remembered every word, and all that went before and came after.

26

EXT. WEXFORD STRAWBERRY FAIR.
AFTERNOON.

A field, in sunshine. A large manor house in the background. The field is crowded with people, country folk dressed for the occasion. There are many stalls selling a variety of fruits, vegetables, free-range eggs, etc. In one corner, a maypole and swings and a bouncy castle, with children playing.

On a bandstand, a brass band is playing 'The Boys of Wexford'. Also seated on the platform are various priests and civic dignitaries. As the band finishes playing, there is polite applause and a man wearing a chain steps forward and calls for silence.

MAN WITH CHAIN

Please, ladies and gentlemen, could I have your attention? Bitta hush, please.

Parents collect their children and hush them down. People move nearer to the stage, among them Dermot and

Tara. Elsewhere in the crowd are Eric and Liam.

MAN WITH CHAIN

(Continuing) Now, I'm not going to make a speech.

Facetious applause. The man with the chain smiles good-humouredly.

MAN WITH CHAIN

(Continuing) It's my very pleasant task here today to announce the presentation of the coveted Tregorran Bowl, for the best strawberries in the County Wexford. Which, by definition, means the best strawberries in the world.

(Applause and cheers)
So to announce the winner and present the award, it's my pleasure and privilege to introduce the honorary president of the Wexford Strawberry Fair – Sir Myles Tregorran!

Sir Myles, a jovial bon viveur in his late sixties, steps forward and nods to the crowd, acknowledging their

28

applause. He takes the envelope from the Man with the Chain, puts on his glasses and extracts a paper, smiling benignly at the audience as he unfolds it.

SIR MYLES

And the winner is... er...

He holds the paper close and squints at it, then holds it at arm's length.

SIR MYLES

(Continuing) Mr Dermot Day, of Downhill Farm.

Cut to Dermot and Tara. Cheers break out and people turn to look at them and clap their backs. Tara is over the moon, Dermot more restrained.

SIR MYLES (O.S.)

Hope to God he's here. Is he?

TARA

Go on, Dermot!

DERMOT

No, this is your job. *(He pushes her)* Go on.

Tara, very fetching in her best garden-party dress, walks to the stage and up the wooden steps, to applause and whistles.

SIR MYLES

(As she arrives) Congratulations, my dear.

He hands her the bowl and, as she takes it, embraces her rather more warmly than he ought, kissing her on both cheeks.

Then, as she holds up the silver bowl and smiles at the gathering, he kisses her again.

Cut to Liam and Eric, in the crowd.

ERIC

Randy oul' goat.

LIAM

I heard that all right.

ERIC

Famous for it. He'd get up on a cracked plate.

LIAM

Isn't he the lucky man he's able?

Tara, on stage, with the bowl, Sir Myles's arm round her waist. She looks straight down at Dermot and blows him a kiss.

Show Dermot, looking proudly back.

* * *

'Clap, for fuck's sake,' said Dick, under his breath, as the audience looked at the freeze frame of Tara gazing out from the onstage monitor.

And sure enough, they did.

'There's love now,' said Michael. 'Across a crowded field.'

'We had a marvellous party that day, after the shoot,' said Linda. 'Didn't we, Conor?'

She was standing beside him, looking up. He pulled her head in to his shoulder.

'Us and half of Wexford,' he said. 'Cast of thousands.'

'And I don't even like strawberries,' said Linda, remembering.

In fact, the day they shot that scene was one of her best memories. One that, to this day, she often conjured up before she went to sleep…

The shooting had ended early but, an hour later, no-one had left.

It was always the same when the extras were real people. They never wanted to go home. They wanted to be able to say later how they had met Dermot and Tara and Aisling and Luke and old whatshisname who played Sir Myles and that they were all very natural.

Champagne, or something like it, had been served to the platform party and the leading actors, cans of beer to the rest. Press photographers were busy lining up shots of Linda, holding the bowl, and old Godfrey, who played Sir Myles, holding Linda.

'That's lovely Linda – just hold that.'

'No, just a minute,' said Linda. 'Where's Conor?'

Everyone looked around, and Conor was pushed forward from his place in the crowd, shaking his head.

'Come on, Conor,' said Linda, pushing the silver bowl into his hands. 'You're the winner.'

Conor took the bowl, put a finger under Linda's chin and kissed her gently.

The cameras snapped away.

'What a pro,' said Eric to Liam, as they sipped their champagne.

'Great,' said the man from the *Herald*.

'Now, could we have one of Linda on her own?'

Conor, relieved, melted into the crowd, where, as the cameras clicked, he stood watching and smiling.

After the shoot, there was a free weekend, and on the Monday morning, before rehearsals began, Conor came to see Lance, as he often did.

Lance's office at that time was on the top floor of the administration block, looking out over the grounds of the TV station. He looked across the cluttered desk at his visitor and spoke mildly enough.

'I'm not sure I understand what you're saying, Conor.'

'It's simple enough,' said Conor. 'I think she has to go.'

Lance sighed, keeping his cool. 'May one ask why?'

'It's the whole feel of the show. It's so bloody cosy. We're all so... settled.'

'You've only been married a year!' Lance broke in, impatiently.

'The audience is bored, I can feel it. We need to shake them up.'

Lance went and stood by the window a moment, then turned, shaking his head.

'It's not on, Conor. They love her.'

Conor interrupted.

'Lance. She goes... or I go. You decide.'

He walked out, leaving the door open.

Tony had a much grander office, in the old Victorian house in whose grounds the studios had been built thirty years earlier. It had a bay window, a high ceiling with its original mouldings, a fine marble fireplace, a sofa in distressed leather and a very large Edwardian partner-desk covered in green leather with gold tooling.

A door led off this room to a kind of pantry, which had been converted to an office for Tony's secretary. This office was filled from from floor to ceiling with box-files of all ages, a table with a big old PC and printer, an even older photocopier and a small typist's desk piled high with papers. In the main office, the magnificent desk had nothing but a telephone. No in-tray, no out-tray, nothing pending.

From the other side of the desk, the visitor's side, Lance watched Tony, hunched in his high-back, leather-feel, multifunctional executive chair, eyes down, toying with a blank sheet of A4 and a pencil, doing one of his long silences. Lance was quite accustomed to this, for Tony had long since turned his producer role into a performance, every move a stage direction. He specialised in immobility, in listening without expression. But he had other moves. The slow, single nod that said, 'Be quiet now, I have the picture.' The slow swivel of the executive chair to look at the opposite wall, which said, 'You're beginning to bore me.' And lately, sudden rages.

Lance too had his box of tricks, including sudden rages, but he never used them with Tony. For Tony, he had perfected an air of the imperturbable, an impression that, whatever life might throw at him, he would keep his cool.

'So it's Conor or Linda?' Tony spoke quietly, without raising his eyes, setting the scene for a sudden rage.

Lance looked out the window.

'There's really no choice, is there?' he said languidly.

Tony snapped his pencil and threw the two parts across the desk. Then he pushed back the executive chair as noisily as he could, walked to the bay window and looked out. Lance, who had seen the move before, waited.

'They haven't had a row, have they?' said Tony. 'I mean, he's still sleeping with her?'

'I believe so. For about six months now. He could be ready to move on.'

'Hardly a reason to write her out, is it?'

He turned, crumpled the piece of A4 and threw it on the carpet.

'Doesn't he realise how popular she is? People are crazy about her!'

Lance did his mirthless smile.

'I think, Tony, that may be the problem.'

This hadn't occurred to Tony but he pretended it had and nodded knowingly.

'Rotten bastard,' he said.

He came back to the desk, splaying fat fingers on the green leather.

'Are you saying we have to do as he says?'

'I'm saying,' said Lance sadly, 'that without Linda, the show can survive. Without Conor, it can't.'

He allowed that to hang in the air a moment, before going on.

'Of course, Tony, if you think we should make a stand, on a matter of principle… we could always kill the show.'

Tony went for the long silence. He had been producer of *The Days* since it began, five years ago. It had taken three months to reach number one in the ratings, but it had remained there ever since.

'Do you think I wouldn't?,' he said.

Lance, who knew he wouldn't, said nothing.

* * *

That week was Aisling's twelfth birthday, and on the studio floor, Lance was rehearsing the party. Tara and Maire and Luke doing their best with a dozen child extras, Aisling in her best frock, preparing to blow out her candles.

'Right, quiet please,' said Lance. 'And… action! Talk, talk, talk!'

The children began to chorus: 'Go on, Ash, you have to!' and Aisling did her shy thing, hanging back, until Tara came and put an arm around her.

'Now come on, Aisling. Big blow!'

'I bet you can't,' said Luke.

Aisling sucked in all the air she could and blew. All but

one went out first time, then the last one. Everyone cheered.

'Now make a wish,' said Tara.

'I wish…' said Aisling, but Tara stopped her.

'No! You mustn't tell!'

Tony, who thought of himself as a hands-on producer, stood on the gallery high above the studio floor, looking down. Conor watched with him. The sound from below barely reached them.

'When does it happen?' said Conor.

'Four weeks,' said Tony.

'Have you told her?'

Tony shook his head.

'Time enough.'

'And what's the story?'

'They're still talking about that,' said Tony. 'You know writers.'

Conor nodded. 'Make it a shocker. Out of the blue. No warning.'

'I've told them that,' said Tony.

'Leak it to the press, but no details. Just 'Downhill's Day of Disaster', that kind of thing. Blow the ratings apart.'

From below, Lance's voice rose, sharper than the others.

'Okay, let's try it again. I want you in quicker Luke, all right? All right, from the top…'

A brief pause, then the voice of Dick: 'Ah, for Christ's sake, somebody light the candles.'

'And by the way,' said Conor. 'I had no part in this.'

'Don't worry, Conor. We'll keep you clean.'

'It's not for myself,' said Conor quickly. 'But if the press got any hint that I was involved, it could be very bad for the show.'

Tony nodded gravely.

'In fact,' Conor went on. 'I'd rather like it to get out that I fought to keep her.'

Tony, not easily shocked, stared at him, and as Conor walked away, gave a slight, disbelieving shake of the head.

The words floated up from below.

'Now, come on, Aisling. Big blow!'

* * *

Back in the theatre, Michael was talking to Linda in a voice of deep concern, as if she had really died.

'As I remember,' he said, 'the next week there was a birthday party?'

Linda nodded. 'Aisling's twelfth.'

'A happy family occasion… and yet, just two or three weeks later…'

'Three.'

'… you were gone.'

'Yes,' said Linda, and sighed. 'But you have to admit, I went out in a blaze of glory.'

'Didn't you just?' said Michael, as he and the audience turned to look at the screen.

EXT. FARMYARD. EVENING.

The haybarn is blazing out of control. Pieces of the blazing structure are falling everywhere. Maire (age 18) stands staring, holding tight to Luke (age 13). Both are weeping and terrified.

Something, perhaps an oil drum, explodes inside and a shower of flames and sparks flies up.

LUKE

(Screams) Ash, where are you? Ash!

CUT TO:

The farm gate, as the truck, returning from the market, drives into the yard. Dermot and Peter jump out.

They shout to be heard above the roar of the fire.

DERMOT

Jesus, Maire, what happened?

MAIRE

Luke and Aisling were up in the loft. They had an oil lamp.

DERMOT

You mean, Aisling...

MAIRE

(Interrupts) She's still inside.

> *As Dermot rips off his coat and turns towards the barn door, Maire grabs his arm.*

MAIRE

(Continuing) Tara too – she went to find her.

> *Dermot runs to the barn, holding his coat over his face, and disappears into the flames.*

MAIRE

(Continuing; screams) Dermot, don't!

PETER

Did you call the fire brigade?

MAIRE

They're on their way. *(Peter runs after Dermot)* Peter, no!

> *As Peter reaches the barn door, Dermot reappears, carrying Aisling, who is coughing and crying, her skin reddened and her clothes charred.*

DERMOT

Take her inside – call the doctor!

> *Dermot runs back into the barn. Peter picks Aisling up and runs with her to Maire, who takes her from him and stumbles towards the house, whispering words of comfort.*

MAIRE

You'll be all right, love.

> *Peter runs back into the barn and Luke stands where he was, staring at the fire. More blazing timbers come crashing down.*

Then the sound of a fire bell and Luke turns to see the first of two fire engines driving into the yard.

The firemen jump down, begin unwinding hoses and connecting them to the water tank in the yard. One drags young Luke back. Another begins to hose down the burning straw around the yard, making sure that the flames don't reach the house.

Others spray water on the barn entrance, trying to clear a path and allow them to see better what is happening inside.

At this point, something is seen emerging from the barn.

FIREMAN

(Shouts) Hold it!

Dermot comes through the smoke and steam, carrying the body of Tara. Peter comes too, and as Tara's head suddenly falls back, he holds it up, staring at it in disbelief.

An ambulance has by now arrived in

the yard. Two paramedics jump out, place Tara on a stretcher and take her into the ambulance. Dermot climbs in after them. Maire runs from the house, her arm around Aisling. They too climb into the ambulance.

DERMOT

(To Peter) Stay with Luke.

Peter nods. The doors of the ambulance close and the ambulance drives out of the yard. End on the burning barn.

EXT. CEMETERY. DAY.

Sombre music. Dermot, Maire, Peter, Luke and Aisling stand by the graveside. Behind, a large number of mourners.

The priest finishes the final decade of the rosary and Dermot throws a flower into the grave. Little Aisling, bandaged, starts to cry and Dermot holds her tight.

3

The audience was quiet for a moment. It hardly seemed proper to applaud.

'You know, of course,' said Michael, 'there wasn't a dry eye in the country.'

Linda smiled.

'Mass protests,' he went on. 'Petitions to let her recover, pictures on the front pages, leading articles even.'

'Yes it was lovely,' said Linda. 'I was dead, but I was really chuffed.'

Michael nodded.

'It must have been a comfort to discover how loved you were.'

'Well, yes, I was amazed. I mean I'd never realised…'

Michael interrupted her.

'So why did it happen?'

She looked puzzled for a moment.

'I mean, why did they kill you off?'

Linda hesitated, and Conor smiled at her

encouragingly. Across the way, in the executive seats, Lance and Tony looked up at the lights.

'Well, you know how it is with soaps,' she said. 'You can't let things become too settled, have to shake people up.'

'Were you sorry to leave?'

'Oh yes,' she said quickly, and looked around her. 'All these people, they were such a joy to work with. We never fell out, did we, Lance?'

From across the stage, Lance smiled at her warmly.

'Never,' he said.

And beside him, Tony nodded agreement.

'It was such a wonderful experience,' she went on. 'And it opened the door to so many things. I learned so much from being part of it. Especially from Conor.'

She took Conor's hand. 'And I know,' she said, 'though he never told me, that he fought very hard to keep me in the show.'

Dick felt it was a moment for applause and the audience obeyed. And across the way, Lance and Tony joined in.

* * *

The wide picture-window of apartment looked upriver, past th far as the Wellington Monument

It was night now and the str

45

the river, growing smaller as they reached into the distance, to Islandbridge and beyond. Conor stood by the window looking out, then came back to sit on the bed. He took Linda's hands and she looked up and smiled, still red-eyed.

'Cheer up,' he said.

'If I could just understand why,' she said. 'I mean all Lance could say was that there was nothing more they could do with the character, that she had reached the end of her natural life. What on earth does that mean?'

Conor shrugged.

'It's the writers,' he said. 'They have this obsession with suffering. Jeopardy. You deliver a tragedy and the audience responds with sympathy. That's the theory. And, of course, if you can make it a spectacular, like this one, so much the better.'

'But why me?' said Linda. 'I was getting great notices. And letters from viewers. I've had hundreds.'

He kissed her hands, said nothing.

'Do you know what's really weird? Getting letters of sympathy on your own death!' She smiled, in spite of herself. 'And, of course, I've had the press on.'

Conor looked a little anxious.

'What did you tell them?'

'Oh, the usual. Parting is such sweet sorrow.'

'You didn't mention Tony? Or Lance?'

'No. How could I? I'd never work again.'

Conor shook his head, overcome by the wickedness of it all.

'I feel like walking out myself,' he said.

'No!'

'I've no heart for it any more.'

'Conor, you mustn't!' She sat up and held his face in her hands. 'It would kill the show! Think of the others!'

'Yes, I suppose…' He lay back beside her, his face close to hers. 'But it won't be the same,' he said. 'The trust is gone you see.'

* * *

'So, yes,' said Linda to Michael. 'I was very sad, but at the same time I was so grateful to Conor for standing by me. And, of course, we've kept in touch, haven't we, darling?'

'Of course we have.'

He kissed her forehead. And, in sitting rooms all around the country, old devotees of *The Days* smiled knowingly.

'Did you see?' they said. 'There was always somethin' between those two. You could always tell.'

'Well, Linda,' said Michael. 'I can only hope that when I'm ten years dead, I'll look as good as you do.'

And he turned to the audience, who were already applauding.

'Ladies and gentlemen – Linda Lee.'

As Dick pumped up the applause into a cheer, Linda

curtsied to the audience, then turned to Conor, who embraced her expertly.

'Bless you, darling,' he said.

She gave a last little bow and took her seat. The applause died and Michael turned a page.

'Life at Downhill Farm resumed its normal course. And for the next eight years, Dermot worked the land and steered his young siblings through the perils of growing up. During those years, there were any number of possible romances, but for Dermot, no-one could take the place of Tara...'

He paused, as a camera zoomed in on Sam, looking arch.

'... until,' he went on, 'early one morning, just as the sun was rising, and Dermot was making his regular trip to the Dublin Fruit Market...'

He turned, and the audience turned with him, to the onstage monitor, on which the busy scene of the Dublin Fruit Market had just come up.

EXT. DUBLIN FRUIT MARKET. DAY.

Early morning. The market is thronged with people. Trucks and vans are drawn up at the entrances to warehouses, loading or unloading fruit, flowers and vegetables.

One of these is Dermot's truck. As Dermot emerges from the warehouse with two empty trays and throws them in the back of the truck, Peter is taking out the last two trays of strawberries, about two dozen half-kilo punnets in each.

DERMOT

Is that the lot?

PETER

Yep.

As Peter goes off to the warehouse, Dermot locks up the tailgate and chats to the man alongside, a large brawny man, unloading six-kilo boxes of tomatoes from the back of a large lorry. The stack of boxes is already nine feet high.

Parked directly in front of this stack is a little Austin Countryman van.

DERMOT

How's she cuttin', Mick?

MICK

No use complainin'.

An attractive girl of nineteen comes out of a door carrying a tray piled high with vegetables. Her name is Lisa Kelly. She is a native of Enniscorthy in County Wexford, where her mother has a fruit and vegetable shop.

She looks nervously around, then heads towards the little Austin Countryman. Not seeing where she is going, she cannons into Dermot. When she speaks, it is with a soft local accent.

LISA

Oh! I'm sorry.

DERMOT

You're all right. Here, let me...

LISA

Ah, no, I'm grand.

She smiles shyly, reaches the little van

and starts loading her produce. Mick
and Dermot watch.

MICK

(Low) I think you're in there, Dermo.

DERMOT

Will you stop!

MICK

I'm tellin' you, now. *(A beat)* Tell us, what
sort of crop had you?

DERMOT

Never better.

MICK

(Rueful) That's the sunny southeast for you.
Up where I am, I had two neighbours wiped
out with the frost.

> *As he talks and stacks his boxes,*
> *Dermot has been watching Lisa. She*
> *closes the back of the van and as she*
> *opens the driver's door, she glances*
> *over. Dermot smiles. She smiles back,*

covered in confusion, closes her door and starts the engine.

Peter, returning with his empty trays, suddenly shouts a warning.

PETER

Watch it!

He is too late. Lisa has backed fast into Mick's stack of tomatoes. The top levels collapse and tomatoes spill all over Lisa's van and the street. Mick jumps off the lorry.

MICK

(Shouts) Ah, you stupid little heifer!

He holds his brawny arms against the stack, saving the lower boxes, but tomatoes are everywhere. Dermot and Peter run to pick up the boxes and get the tomatoes back in.

Lisa jumps out of the van, mortified.

LISA

God, I'm sorry, I thought I was in neutral... Oh, Jesus, I'm really sorry.

She kneels to help.

DERMOT

It's all right now, it's under control.

MICK

Well, Jaze, I'm glad *you're* under control.

Peter jumps up to help Mick, who has his arms around the stack of boxes, straining to keep them upright. Together they manage to get them stable. The fallen boxes are refilled and placed on top.

Lisa looks on helplessly. She takes tomatoes from the roof of her van and puts them in the boxes. Eventually, the last box is put on top, but there are still lots of squashed tomatoes on the ground.

LISA

(To Mick) I'll pay you for what I destroyed.

Mick is about to reply when Dermot breaks in.

DERMOT

Ah, sure there wasn't much damage, was
there Mick? *(Mick glares at him)* Like, it
could have been worse.

MICK

(Deep breath) I suppose I coulda been kilt.

*He bangs the door of his truck and
marches off to the nearby café.*

DERMOT

(To Lisa) He'll be all right. Is this your first
time?

LISA

Wouldn't you know?

DERMOT

But you'll be coming back?

LISA

Yeah, I suppose.

DERMOT

Don't worry. You'll get the hang of it.

PETER

(From the cab of the truck) Come on
Dermot, let's move.

LISA

I don't know what I'd have done without
you.

DERMOT

Forget it.

LISA

D'you come every day?

DERMOT

Mondays and Thursdays.

LISA

I suppose I'll see you again, then?

(Getting into the truck) **Of course you will.
You need looking after.**

*He gives her his special smile and
starts the engine.*

*As the truck backs away, she watches
him go and gives him a little wave.
Smitten.*

* * *

The sun pushed its way up over the Pigeon House and
sent a sliver of early light through the parting of the
curtains in Conor O'Hara's bedroom. At the same
moment, the door opened with a clatter and Conor came
in, wearing a white towelling dressing gown, carrying a
tray with two cups of coffee.

'Wakey, wakey!' he shouted.

And, in the bed, young Samantha Black, looking and
sounding not at all like little Lisa Kelly from Enniscorthy,
sat up, startled and naked.

'Gosh,' she said.

Conor left the tray down and opened the curtains
wide. When he came back to the bed, she was already
drinking her coffee.

'What's the time?'

'Eight,' said Conor.

'So why are you up and about? The call's not till eleven.'

'I like to be early.'

'Yes,' said Sam. 'I heard them saying that. Good old reliable Conor – never late.'

'Not so much of the "old".'

'Sorry,' said Sam. 'Touched a nerve did I?' She looked around the room. 'I never dreamed that this was going to happen.'

And she had done her share of dreaming. No-one would have guessed that Wexford was in fact her native place, that a mere five years ago, she had left the snug town of Gorey as Sheila Duggan, to come back now as Samantha Black, playing little Lisa Kelly, soon to be Lisa Day. No wonder she was confused.

After leaving school, she and her friend Molly had taken the boat and train to London where they offered their services as in-store models in the fashion houses of Oxford Street. They eventually accepted posts as cleaners in John Lewis's, on a purely temporary basis while they looked for an agency that would teach them how to be models. They approached several of these but found that their salaries as cleaners were well below the tuition fees involved. Molly was not as keen on modelling as Sheila. She was happy to settle for being a world-famous actress, and with that in view, she joined the Foster Academy of Dramatic Art in Hampstead and persuaded Sheila to join with her. It was actually in Kentish Town but Hampstead was fairly near and sounded better. And it was quite cheap.

Miss Foster was devoted to the works of Noel Coward and Terence Rattigan, and had a grudging admiration for the works, though not the ways, of Oscar Wilde. To equip them for performing these works, her students were taught a clipped form of speech with tortured vowel sounds and an air of *ennui*. At the end of their course, they were given diplomas and recommendations to a repertory company in Essex, run by Miss Foster's younger brother. And so it came that Sheila and Molly, now Samantha and Michelle, began their stage careers.

They were not the most glamorous careers. Philip Foster (72) owned the theatre, which held eighty, but the houses were surprisingly good, considering how little the repertoire changed. No matter how often they revived *Blithe Spirit*, they always packed for three weeks, with the same audience in the wine bar afterwards, marking tonight's performance against last year's.

The company's four juvenile leads, as they were called, shared a small flat in Chingford. The other two were from somewhere in northern England, but since they too had been taught by Miss Foster, all four sounded exactly the same.

They got on well, drinking hot wine together after the show, telling stories of their youth. The other two would shriek with laughter to hear that there was really a place in Ireland called Gorey. 'How sweet,' they chorused.

But Sam had realised that this was not the way ahead. She knew how important it was to have an agent, but no London agent was interested. So she collected her notices from the local paper and sent them, with an imaginative CV and a set of seductive photographs, to an agent in Dublin. For almost a year she heard nothing, then, out of the blue, she had a letter saying that she had been put up for a starring role in *The Days of Downhill Farm*, the show which, every Sunday night, as a little girl, she had been allowed to stay up and watch.

And she had been called for audition! There was a real chance to become the TV wife of the legendary Conor O'Hara! And with her looks, and her Wexford background, said the agent, she had a real chance!

But this, thought Sam, could be the problem. It was four years since she had spoken Wexford.

The audition, in Dublin, was a week away. Sam phoned Mr Foster to tell him, in a broken voice, that her father had died in Ireland and that she must hurry home. This was not entirely untrue, for her father had indeed died in Ireland, ten years previously. Michelle, her understudy, would take over the part of Cecily in *The Importance of Being Earnest*. And Sam spent the next week in Gorey, practising her Wexford accent with her mother, sisters and friends.

At the audition, she bowled Lance over, and now, at last, here she was, a star. In Conor O'Hara's bed. Naked.

Conor put his coffee down and stroked her shoulder.

'You know the marriage is set for June the first?'

'I heard a rumour.' She sipped her coffee before going on. 'Actually, I heard another rumour.'

'Yes?'

'About the lovely Linda. I heard a whisper that you and she were quite close in real life.'

'Oh, I've heard that one too. It's good for the show, that kind of gossip.'

She looked at him archly.

'Do you ever see her now?'

'Oh, we keep in touch,' he said. 'I make a point of ringing her from time to time, see how she's faring. I'm very fond of her.'

Sam nodded gravely.

'And they're really going to marry us off?'

'That's the plan.'

'Aren't you just a little old for me?'

He decided not to take the bait.

'Well, you know what they say,' he said. 'If you're big enough…'

'Yes, yes, stop boasting,' she said, cutting him short.

He took the cup from her, put it on the tray and put the tray on the floor.

'But you could be right,' he said. 'I may be a bit rusty.' He climbed between the sheets. 'Maybe what I need… is a little more rehearsal.'

He took her in his arms and she giggled.

'Oh, Mr Day,' she said, using her Lisa voice, 'Aren't you a desperate man entirely?'

* * *

It had been a good night at the Café Vangelis. The exodus, for taxis and last buses, was under way.

'Good night. Thank you,' said Rose, as a couple left.

'Good night, Queenie,' they called.

And the little unseen lady in the kitchen called back, 'Good night, love. Safe home.'

Rose took the remains of their dinner on her tray and took it to the hatch, then crossed to the table where Conor sat alone, before an empty wine bottle and a half-full glass, yawning.

'Are you sleepy?' asked Rose.

'Mm…' said Conor. 'Been hard at it all day.'

'No rest for the wicked,' said Rose. 'Would you like a sweet?'

Conor shook his head. 'Watchin' the figure.'

'Coffee?'

'Not tonight, Rose, thank you. Just the bill.'

As she began to write, another couple were making their way to the door.

'Good night, Queenie,' they called. 'See ya.'

And again the voice from the kitchen. 'Good night, love. Mind yourself!'

'Who is this Queenie?' said Conor.

Rose was still calculating.

'Me mother,' she said. 'Does the cookin', takes the money, runs the show.'

'And those two?' said Conor, nodding at the other two waitresses who sat gossiping at a table opposite.

'Phil and Gina. Mam's young sisters. All in the family, you see.'

She put the bill on the saucer, gave him her best smile and went off.

Conor glanced at the bill, took out two twenties and left them on the saucer.

He finished his glass of wine and stood up. Then, glancing towards the kitchen, he changed his mind, lifted the bill and the money and walked over. Arriving at the hatch, he saw a dark woman in a blue smock, standing with her back to him, scraping food from a bowl into a waste bucket. And whistling.

He coughed, and she turned and saw him.

'That's a bad cough you have,' she said.

She was small, pretty, feisty, pushing forty. And it was plain to Conor, who was experienced in these matters, that she had no idea who he was.

'I believe you're Queenie,' he said.

'No use denyin' it'.

'I'm Conor,' he said, offering his hand.

She raised her little red hands to her shoulders and wiggled them.

'I'm after filletin' a haddock,' she said.

Conor grinned. 'Fair enough.'

He handed over the bill and the money and she opened the cash register.

'The lamb was wonderful,' he told her.

Queenie was counting out change, mouthing the figures, showing small, white teeth.

'Oh, it's amazin' what you can do with a bit of oul' wether mutton,' she said, 'if you have the right hammer.'

As she spoke, she was putting the change in the saucer. A fiver and four pound coins. He took the coins and left the fiver.

'Oh, God, you musta liked it,' said Queenie.

'Didn't I tell you!'

Queenie interrupted him.

'You're very good,' she said. 'But listen, why don't you give it to little Rose there, she'll be made up.'

She put the note in his hand, and he nodded.

'If you say so. Good night, Queenie.'

'Safe home, now,' she said, and went back to scraping the bowl.

On his way to the door, Conor stopped by Rose and slipped her the fiver.

'Oh, thanks a mill.'

'Good night, Rose,' said Conor and backed out expertly.

Rose, wreathed in smiles, looked at Phil and Gina.

'Isn't he lovely?' she said.

* * *

In the television theatre, Michael was speaking to the audience with the air of one making a surprising announcement.

'And so,' he declaimed, 'almost four years ago, Dermot Day married sweet innocent Lisa…'

Sam smiled brilliantly as the camera zoomed in.

'… and brought her back to Downhill Farm, where, almost immediately, nature took its course.'

He turned to the onstage monitor, as the picture came up of the kitchen garden at Downhill Farm.

4

EXT. KITCHEN GARDEN/DOWNHILL FARM. DAY.

Lisa, heavily pregnant, is taking clothes off the line. She puts them in a basket which is already very full, bends and picks it up, and starts towards the house.

DERMOT (O.S.)

Lisa! What are you doing?

He comes into shot and takes the basket from her.

DERMOT

Are you crazy?

LISA

There's no need to go mad. I'm well able to do it.

DERMOT

(Sees she is upset) I'm sorry, love, I'm just worried about you. Go inside now and rest.

LISA

That's all I do. I'll go mad sittin' in there, lookin' at the wall.

DERMOT

Just… put your feet up. Read a book.

He kisses her. She turns away, still sulky.

LISA

I'm goin' for a walk.

She walks away towards the front yard. Dermot follows with the laundry basket. A voice off-stage is heard calling.

Post!

EXT. FARMYARD/DOWNHILL. MORNING.

Luke and Aisling are seen coming from the gate with a bundle of post. The postman is seen cycling out through the gate.

The rest of the family come to meet them, Dermot and Lisa from the garden, Maire from the house, Peter from the barn.

The pile of post includes magazines, catalogues, etc., which their recipients grab as Luke calls out their names.

LUKE

Bill, bill, bill... *(He hands these to Dermot)* Maire, Peter.

He sniffs the pink envelope before Peter grabs it from him.

LUKE

(Continuing) Now what's this? *(A yellow envelope with gold edging)*
Mr and Mrs Dermot Day.

LISA

Thank you.

> *She plucks it from his hand, opens it and pulls out an embossed invitation card, studies it a moment.*

LISA

(Continuing) Oh listen to this… *(Adopts a posh voice)* Sir Myles Tregorran requests the company of Mr and Mrs Dermot Day, at a Garden Party at 3pm on Saturday the twentieth of August, in celebration of his engagement… *(All exchange wide-eyed looks)* to the Honourable Daphne Symington-Travers of The Grange, Whittenfield-in-the-Hollow, Dorset.

PETER

Well, Holy Divine God!

LUKE

Engagement?

AISLING

Sure he must be eighty.

MAIRE

Indeed'n he's not!

PETER

Well, he's over seventy.

AISLING

Sure, who would have him?

MAIRE

Plenty. Hasn't he all the money in the world?

DERMOT

(To Lisa) Do you want to go?

LISA

Ah, would you look at me, how could I go?
But *you* must.

DERMOT

On a Saturday? *(Shakes his head)* I'll be on the road all day.

MAIRE

You have to. You can't insult the man.

AISLING

And we want to hear all the dirt.

Peter and Luke join in, telling him he has to go.

DERMOT

Well, I'll see how things go. If I get the deliveries done, I might drop in. You coming, Lisa?

LISA

In a minute.

She kisses his cheek and he goes off to the house, carrying the laundry basket.

AISLING

I wonder what she's like.

LUKE

Who?

AISLING

The one he's marryin'. Daphne Pot-Noodle
or whatever her name is.

LUKE

Prob'ly as old as the hills.

AISLING

I wouldn't say so. I remember Sir Myles
comin' to give out the prizes at school and
he groped everybody in sixth year.

MAIRE

Aisling, will you show some respect!

AISLING

It's true. I bet you she's some young one.

LUKE

And she'll kill him in six months!

PETER

(Grins) Great way to go, all the same!

MAIRE

God, you're all disgusting.

AISLING

Well, if she is a young one, she's disgusting too. Imagine sleepin' with somebody that's old enough to be your father.

A little silence at this.

LISA

Yeah, just imagine.

She turns and walks away to the house. Everybody looks askance at Aisling. She puts a hand to her mouth.

AISLING

I didn't mean that. And anyway it's not the same. (*A beat. No-one speaks*) It's nothin' like the same...

The others shake their heads and walk away from her.

* * *

'Tell me about your new bride,' said Linda.

They were in Conor's apartment. Linda had cooked dinner and they were finishing the wine.

'She's a little young, isn't she?' said Conor.

'I would have thought you might enjoy that,' she said.

'I preferred my first wife.'

'Such an old charmer.' But she wanted to hear more. 'She's pretty,' she said.

He shook his head. 'Not in the same league.'

'If you really mean that, why are we like this?'

'Like what?'

'Hiding away, like criminals.'

'But I love that, shutting out the world.'

'Conor, how long is it since I left the show?'

'Who's counting?'

'Almost eight years. And look at us. Why can't we ever go out, like a normal couple?'

'You know why.'

'I don't. Really. Tell me.'

'Well, for a start, there's Freddy.'

'As you well know, Conor, Freddy and I share a house, two cars and several credit cards, nothing else... And he knows how things are.'

'People talk, Linda.'

'Who cares? We've nothing to be ashamed of.'

'Yes, but there's the show.'

She stared at him.

'The viewers.'

She looked away and he took her hand.

'They're important, Linda. At the moment, they have to think of Dermot and Lisa as real people, starting out on a new life together. If they could see me now, having it off with the ex-wife…'

She put a hand to his mouth. 'Conor, I know you like to think of it all as real, but it isn't. Honestly.'

'I know it isn't. But the people out there believe it. If it was to get out that you and I were still… you know… eight years after your death…'

'Yes?'

'Well, they'd lose faith.'

She looked at him, wide-eyed.

'They'd think of me as cheating on my new, pregnant wife. Don't you see? That just isn't Dermot.'

* * *

EXT. TREGORRAN HALL. DAY.

Open on the Hall, a fine stately home, as Dermot's rather shabby truck drives through the front gate and up the drive.

Reaching the wide steps that lead up to the grand entrance, he parks the old truck alongside the row of

Jaguars, elderly sports cars and shining new Range Rovers. As he gets out, he is seen to be in his working clothes – moleskin trousers, open-neck shirt and old tweed jacket. An old retainer comes to meet him. He speaks respectfully at first, but on recognising Dermot, lapses quickly into the vernacular.

RETAINER

Afternoon, sir.

DERMOT

How'r'ya Seamus?

RETAINER

Oh, Jaze, Dermot it's yourself. Are you here for the hooley?

DERMOT

The tail end of it. Where are they?

RETAINER

The Hibiscus Garden.

DERMOT

The wha'?

RETAINER

Round the back. You can't miss them.

DERMOT

Right. Watch that vehicle now. I don't want anybody liftin' it.

RETAINER

(As Dermot goes off) I'd say you'll be safe enough.

Dermot grins as he heads towards the corner of the house.

EXT. THE HIBISCUS GARDEN. DAY.

About forty guests are in the garden, all in smart – if slightly dated – casual clothes, blazers and flouncy summer dresses. Maids of all ages carry trays of fizzy wine and canapés.

Dermot appears round the gable, stops to take things in, takes a deep

*breath and sets off across the lawn,
attracting the odd raised eyebrow
from other guests.*

*He is heading for the bench where Sir
Myles, eight years older than when
last seen, sits on a bench quaffing
champagne and chatting to others of
his own vintage.*

*Sir Myles sees Dermot coming, gets to
his feet and pumps his hand.*

SIR MYLES

It's young Day. How good of you to come.

DERMOT

Good of you to ask me, Sir Myles.

SIR MYLES

Haven't you brought the little woman?

DERMOT

I'm afraid, sir, she's on the verge of a happy
event.

SIR MYLES

Oh, I say, well done! Congratulations!

DERMOT

And to you. *(He looks around)* I'm looking forward to meeting your fiancée.

SIR MYLES

And so you shall! *(Shouts)* Daphne!

> *Daphne, chatting to a group nearby, turns and gives a dazzling smile.*

SIR MYLES

(Continuing) Come and meet our neighbour!

> *She comes to join them. She is attractive, aristocratic and gamey, a little younger than Dermot.*

SIR MYLES

(Continuing) Daphne, this is Day. Day – Daphne.

DAPHNE

(Taking him off) How d'ye do, Day?

DERMOT

(Grins) It's Dermot.

DAPHNE

Yes, I knew that. Myles has told me all about you. Have you seen our azaleas?

DERMOT

Well, no...

DAPHNE

Come, I'll show you.

Quite unselfconsciously, she takes his hand and leads him to the shrubbery. Sir Myles, smiling proudly, watches them go.

* * *

Conor and Linda lay close together, scarcely moving. They had made love, as always, in a kind of slow motion, full of pleasure, but always in control. And when it was over, he stayed close. It was a part of his technique that the critics always praised, his attention to detail.

Their lips brushed together, feeling each other's breath.

'What about the new one?' said Linda.

He looked puzzled, though he knew what she meant. She knew he knew, but she explained anyway.

'The lady of the manor,' she said.

'Well, I hardly know her.'

'She's quite a looker.'

'Oh, she's great casting,' said Dermot. 'It's the voice, you see, the upper-crust thing, you can't fake that. And the gear, the arse in the jodhpurs. People find that very sexy.'

Linda nodded. 'Lady Chatterley.'

'That's it.'

'And will Dermot be playing the gamekeeper?'

'It's looking that way.'

'Lucky old Der–'

He put a finger on her lips. 'Why must we always be talking about the show?'

'We don't have to. What would you like to talk about?'

'Well…' He thought about it. 'You. Your life and times.'

'Oh, God, don't ask.' She moved away a little.

'What's up?'

'Well, you know we were buying this place in Spain?'

He nodded.

'We had two or three places lined up to inspect and we were booked to go out next month. Two weeks, five-star hotel.'

'Wouldn't knock it.'

'Except that Freddy can't come now. Business. He's going to Japan.'

'*You* can still go, can't you?'

'Yes, I suppose…' She pulled him close again. 'It's not that I'd miss him. But you need somebody across the table.' She stroked his hair. 'Why don't you come?'

He said nothing.

'I wish you could.'

He still said nothing.

'But I don't suppose they'd let you,' she said.

* * *

In his eyrie in the old house, Tony snapped his pencil and threw the two bits across his desk.

'What in Christ's name do you mean?'

'Exactly what I say,' said Conor. 'I'm taking time off.'

Lance looked at the wall.

Tony was already in position at the window, facing out.

'You're not, you know,' he said, not turning round.

'Two weeks from the twenty-fourth,' said Conor, matter-of-factly. 'Episodes twenty-nine and thirty.'

Tony turned from the window, filled with quiet menace.

'It's out of the fucking question,' he said.

'Perhaps, Conor, you'd tell us why,' said Lance, pouring oil.

'Of course,' said Conor. 'Medical advice.'

'Ah,' said Tony. 'And perhaps you'd tell us what the fuck ails you?'

'I've been having blackouts. Blood pressure... something. My doctor advises me that if I don't get away – a period of complete rest – he can't be responsible.'

He walked to the door and opened it. As always, he was perfectly rehearsed.

'I'll get you a medical certificate of course.'

'You walk out that door now,' roared Tony, 'and you'll never work again!'

'No, wait,' said Lance.

He went to Conor and put his arm around him.

'Conor, we're perfectly happy to give you time off. God knows, your health is as important to us as it is to you. If you could just give us more time. You're in all the stories, the scripts are written.'

'Rewrite them,' said Conor. He seemed surprised that they had not seen this solution. 'What are writers for?'

He left, closing the door quietly behind him.

'Christ,' said Tony.

EXT. THE SHRUBBERY, TREGORRAN HALL. DAY.

A narrow winding path between high bushes of azalea and rhododendron, almost a maze. Dermot and Daphne appear round a bend, walking hand in hand.

DAPHNE

Wonderful blooms, don't you think?

DERMOT

Hm. Make a wonderful bouquet. *(She smiles roguishly)* When is it to be?

DAPHNE

We haven't set a date. Myles wants it to be as soon as possible. *(Dermot nods innocently)* Oh, I know what you're thinking. Old man in a hurry. No time to waste.

DERMOT

(Grinning) No, I wasn't.

DAPHNE

Yes, you were. I know what they're all thinking.

DERMOT

Tell me.

DAPHNE

Well, you know the old song. *(She sings)* 'Her beauty was sold, For an old man's gold, She's a bird in a gilded cage.'

She gives a little peal of laughter and leans her head against his chest, then rearranges her features.

DAPHNE

(Continuing) I'm actually very fond of him.

Dermot nods gravely.

DERMOT

Have you known each other long?

DAPHNE

Oh, yes. Since I was quite small. He and Daddy served together in the war.

Dermot opens his mouth to say something, then closes it. She gives him a friendly punch.

DAPHNE

(Continuing) You were going to say 'Which one?' weren't you?

DERMOT

(Grinning) No, I wasn't.

DAPHNE

Yes, you were! Well I don't care what people say. Never did.

Her mood changes, as it frequently does.

DAPHNE

(Continuing) I'm really looking forward to living in Ireland.

DERMOT

D'you have many friends here?

DAPHNE

Well, I have you. *(She squeezes his arm)* And
I've been over quite often. For the hunting.
And the Horse Show. Do you hunt?

DERMOT

(Deep breath) As it happens, no.

DAPHNE

We'll have to change that won't we?

They emerge from the shrubbery.

EXT. THE HIBISCUS GARDEN. DAY.

*As they emerge, Daphne stops and
stares.*

DAPHNE

Oh Lord! Intruders!

*Dermot looks and sees Luke and
Aisling. They have reached the gable
of the house on Luke's motorbike,
thrown it on the grass and are
hurrying across the lawn. Seamus, the*

old retainer, is seen struggling after them, remonstrating.

DERMOT

(Shouts) Luke!

They turn and run towards him.

DERMOT

(To Daphne) It's my brother.

LUKE

(Arrives, out of breath) It's Lisa...

AISLING

She's started.

LUKE

Peter's taken her to the hospital.

DERMOT

Jesus! *(To Daphne)* Look, I'm sorry, I have to go.

DAPHNE

Yes, of course.

DERMOT

(Interrupts) It's my wife, she's...

DAPHNE

Yes, I understand. Now hurry!

> *She squeezes his hands and he turns and hurries off with Luke and Aisling. Sir Myles has wandered over to join Daphne. They watch as the other three run off.*

DAPHNE

(Continuing) Mr Day had to leave. He said to say goodbye.

SIR MYLES

Dam' bad form.

> *Stay on Daphne's face as she watches Dermot disappearing. Meanwhile, Sir Myles drones on in the background.*

SIR MYLES (O.S.)

... Turns up looking like a stableboy, then runs off without so much as a kiss-my-arse...

5

As the picture faded from the screen and Dick called for applause, Michael turned again to Conor.

'And, in fact,' he said, 'Dad arrived at the hospital just in time for the birth. The dawn, so to speak, of a new Day.'

The audience groaned, but he pressed on.

'So it was all happening,' he said. 'The birth of your baby, the arrival of the beautiful Daphne, obviously hellbent on seducing you. And suddenly Dermot disappears. What was that all about?'

Conor smiled enigmatically. 'I fell ill,' he said.

'Ah, yes, we all saw that. The sudden collapse, the midnight trip to the hospital. But why? There was no build-up, no follow-up. Two weeks later you were back, large as life.'

'But it was true,' said Conor. 'And the truth doesn't always make a good story.'

'You mean, you really were ill?'

Conor hesitated.

'I think I just… needed a rest. I mean, I'd been in every episode since day one, not a day off in twelve years. I started having the odd blackout, and they were getting more and more frequent. So I went for a checkup and the doctor was… well, a little concerned. Said something about vaso-vagal attacks. I'm still not sure what they are, but he did say that I had to take a proper rest, get away from pressure.

'Three months, he said. And, of course, that was impossible. But I realised that if I were to have a real breakdown, well… what would happen to the show? And all the people who worked on it.'

He shrugged.

'So I met him halfway. I took two weeks.'

You could feel the waves of admiration rolling up from the audience. There was even an unprovoked ripple of applause.

'Still,' said Michael. 'It must have been something of a crisis for the show?'

'Yes, but they were very good about it,' said Conor.

Tony and Lance smiled faintly.

'They'd have had to tweak the scripts a bit, change the stories. They couldn't tell me exactly what they'd do, but they told me not to worry. Just to go off, forget about the show for a couple of weeks and get well.'

'Which, of course, you did. Where did you go, by the way?'

'Trinidad,' said Conor.

It came out so naturally that Linda blinked at first, but she recovered quickly.

'It was wonderful just to lie in the sun, look at the sky, swim a little. Best of all, no-one knew me. Well, one or two looked at me strangely... you know the way... where have we seen him before? But they didn't bother me.'

'And yet,' said Michael, 'When the cat was away...'

Conor smiled ruefully.

Sam's voice piped up: 'Oh, no! You're not going to show that?'

'Oh, yes we are!'

He turned to the audience.

'Shall we see what was happening back on the farm?'

Cries of approval came from the audience as they looked up at the screen.

EXT. DOWNHILL FARM. RIVERBANK.

Open on the river, the sun shining on it.

It is a blazing-hot summer's day. Peter, Luke, Aisling and Lisa lie on the bank sunbathing and drinking cider. Peter and Luke are stripped to the waist, Lisa and Aisling in bikini tops and shorts. Baby Stephen is in a basket, protected from the sun.

LUKE

You not visiting today, Lisa?

LISA

After tea. They like him to sleep in the
afternoons.

AISLING

Just as well he can't see us now, he'd have a
relapse.

*Peter reaches for the bottle. He looks
at it, finds it empty.*

PETER

Hey what's this?

LISA

Not me, I'm on the dry.

*Peter looks at Luke, who is draining a
glass.*

PETER

All right, Luke. There's another bottle in the
fridge. Go and get it.

LUKE

Why me?

PETER

Now! Go on.

LUKE

Yeah, yeah. Come on, Ash.

Aisling gets up and they go off up the hill towards the house. Peter watches them go, shakes his head.

PETER

Too fond of the sauce, that fella.

He lies down again, alongside Lisa, whose eyes are closed. Peter watches her a moment, spots a buttercup and plucks it.

He gets up on one elbow, leans over her and holds the buttercup under her chin, his face close to hers.

She opens her eyes, startled. Peter smiles down at her.

PETER

(Continuing) I'd say you like butter.

He kisses her. She turns her face away immediately, shocked.

LISA

What are you doing?

He kisses her again. This time she stays a moment, then breaks away again.

LISA

(Continuing) No!

He holds her face, gently enough, and kisses her again. This time she responds. The kiss becomes more passionate and she puts an arm around his neck.

Then again she breaks away, says an even louder 'No' and sits up.

PETER

Why not?

LISA

Because I don't want to.

PETER

It didn't seem that way...

LISA

(Interrupts) All right, I let you, I shouldn't
have, but no more. I won't do anything to
hurt Dermot.

PETER

How can it hurt him? He doesn't know.

LISA

I could tell him.

PETER

Why? *(A beat)* What's the harm?

    *Lisa is angry, as much with herself as
with Peter.*

LISA

He's done so much for you. And this is how you pay him back!

PETER

Oh, come on, Lisa. *(A beat)* He's twice your age.

LISA

(Interrupts, really angry) How dare you say that! He's the best, straightest man who ever lived, and you want me to cheat on him – his own brother!

PETER

(A deep breath) Look, forget it, okay?

LISA

At least he's grown-up, not a spoilt child.

> *He lay on his back now, his head turned away. A beat.*

LISA

(Continuing) I'm sorry, I shouldn't have said that.

No reply. She leans over him.

LISA

(Continuing) **Peter? I'm sorry.**

PETER

(Turns to her) **No, I was wrong.**

> **As the mutual apologies go on, they kiss again and this time it is mutual and for real. He pulls her down, then turns over so that his body covers hers.**

* * *

As the picture faded, a low 'Ooo... ooh' rose from the actors sitting in the rows behind Sam, and the audience joined in. Michael looked severely at Lisa.

'I hope you were thoroughly ashamed,' he said.

Sam hung her head.

'It was a moment of madness,' she said.

'What did you think of it all Conor?'

'Well, of course,' said Conor, 'I was incommunicado. Knew nothing about it. I remember coming back from my holiday, people at the airport telling me how glad they were to see me. They thought I might be dead, you see. Now at that stage, the scene at the river had been filmed, but it hadn't been screened. So I had no idea what was going on until I got home, picked up the scripts and read them.'

'And what did you think?'

Conor hesitated. And across the stage, Tony and Lance watched each other from the corners of their eyes.

'I thought they were wonderful,' he said.

* * *

Conor, heavily tanned, threw open the door and flung the script on the green, tooled leather of Tony's executive desk.

'What the fuck do you think you're doing?' he said.

'Welcome back, Conor,' murmured Lance.

Conor ignored him, concentrated on Tony.

'Well?' he said.

'What exactly is your complaint?' said Tony mildly.

'This!' he shouted, picking up the script, crushing it in his hands.

'We thought it was rather good, didn't we Lance?'

'It makes me look like a fucking idiot.'

He threw the script down again. He would have liked to think of another move, but in Tony's bare office there were few props.

'A new wife who's supposed to worship me – having it off with my young brother! How do you think it makes me look?'

'Conor, you weren't there. You didn't look like *anything*.'

'And this line, look! Look!'

He was flipping through the pages, getting nowhere. He gave up.

'Peter's line. That I'm twice her age!'

'It's just a figure of speech,' said Lance.

'It isn't even true!'

'Look, Conor.' Lance was placatory. 'At the time you... er... fell ill, you were in all the stories, then suddenly we didn't have you. We had to rewrite, at short notice. We needed a story without you and this is what the writers...'

'Don't!' Conor held a hand up. 'Just don't mention those useless fuckers! I haven't missed an episode in twelve years and now, when I ask for time off, when my back is turned – this is what they do!'

Tony intervened. 'For Christ's sake, Conor, it's a great story. Everybody's talking about it. The episode you reappear – little Lisa with the guilty secret. Will she tell you, won't she tell you? You'll have all the sympathy...'

Conor broke in. 'You mean, they'll feel sorry for me?'

Tony rolled his eyes up.

Conor blazed on. 'Can't you see? Either of you? It's not my character! Dermot is not the kind of person that this happens to!'

Tony and Lance looked dumbly at each other. Conor took the script off the desk and threw it on the floor.

'It can't go out,' he said.

Tony spoke from his leather-feel chair.

'The show's recorded, it's edited and it goes out on Sunday.'

'You have to pull it,' said Conor.

'Not possible.'

Before Conor could speak, Lance came in.

'Conor, from the moment you return, we'll do it your way. The sun will shine out of your arse.'

'She has to confess,' said Conor. 'On her knees. And Dermot will forgive her. And take her back. He's that sort of person.'

Tony and Lance nodded solemnly.

Conor walked to the door. 'I want script clearance.'

They nodded.

'In writing.'

They nodded again.

He left.

EXT. DOWNHILL FARM. THE ORCHARD.
DAY.

Lisa and Dermot stand under a tree. A basket is on the ground, half-filled with fruit. Lisa, having finished her confession, stands with her head down.

LISA

I'll never forgive myself.

Dermot puts a hand under her chin,
turns her face up.

DERMOT

It's all right, it's all right. You didn't need to tell me but you did. It's over now.

LISA

I was missing you so much. I wanted someone to be close to and he... he was just there. I just closed my eyes and tried to think of you...

He puts an arm around her. She looks
up at him.

LISA

(Continuing) You won't ever be able to trust me again. But it won't ever happen again, I promise.

DERMOT

I know it won't. Stop blaming yourself.

LISA

Will you say anything to Peter?

Dermot shakes his head.

DERMOT

It's in the past. Let it stay there.

She leans her head on his chest and holds him close.

LISA

I don't deserve you.

* * *

'A saint,' said Michael to the studio audience. 'A walking saint.'

He turned to Conor, who was grinning sheepishly.

'And so, all ended happily. Conor went back to his raspberries and Lisa to her beautiful baby.'

Right on cue, little Stephen looked into the lens and burped.

'But, of course, he's only borrowed, isn't he?'

Sam nodded. 'Rent-a-Child,' she said.

A voice spoke from the row behind. It was Eve Staunton, who played Maire.

'Actually, he's mine,' she said.

Sam lifted Stephen and rubbed noses.

'Would you like to go to Mummy?' she said, in her best baby-talk. 'Yes, of course you would.'

She passed Stephen back over her head, then took a tissue from a box and wiped her hands, getting a small laugh.

'Family show, you see,' said Michael to the audience. 'They share everything.'

'In fact,' he added, with the air of one sharing a confidence, not only is Stephen's mum part of the show, but so too is his dad, who is in fact with us tonight. But I won't mention his name, for fear of embarrassing him.'

By now, a camera had rushed to get a shot of the unfortunate Dick, who closed his eyes as the cast stood up and applauded him. As the audience began to join in, Dick, determined to remain in character, scowled fiercely and made the stern breast-stroke gesture that said stop.

Michael looked sympathetically at Eve.

'He's like this at home is he?' he asked.

'No, never,' said Eve, wide-eyed. 'He's as quiet as a mouse. Never swears, never raises his voice.'

She was lying, of course, and the cast around her raised their eyebrows and giggled.

The others in the cast generally liked being in *The Days*. They would complain of how it tied them down, and how they could never get time off to work in the theatre, or film even. But the money was good, as were the recognition and the perks. When the big movie offer came, they could walk away, but until then, hey – don't knock it.

Eve was the exception. She hated it, and most of all she hated the character she played. Maire, the eternal elder sister, the rock of sense. Always keeping the others, Peter, Luke and Aisling, on a steady course, handing out boring advice, heading for tight-lipped spinsterhood.

At home, with Dick, she actually swore far more than he did. They had met on the show, and they were drawn to each other by their shared dislike, not only of Lance and Tony and Conor, but of the show itself, and even the entire rotten pus-filled world of showbusiness. But it gave them three incomes. (Even little Stephen was self-supporting.) And they had a long-term plan to buy a pub on the Costa Blanca, which they would call The Funky Worm. They had been saving hard for this. Another year of *The Days* would have done it.

Michael was already walking upstage to where the guests made their entrance.

'And now,' he declaimed, 'from the newest arrival at Downhill Farm, we turn to its oldest inhabitants.'

Backstage, waiting to be called, stood Eric and Liam, and alongside them, a pretty, slightly distraught researcher, holding a clipboard, listening to Michael's introduction, waiting for the cue from the voice onstage.

'Fifty years ago,' it said, 'these two young brothers arrived at Downhill Farm to work for Dermot's father. Ten years on, he converted one of the stable buildings on the farm and they moved in. When Dermot took over, he hadn't the heart to shift them, so they're still there.'

Backstage, the researcher whispered to Eric, 'Isn't he marvellous?'

'Who?' said Eric, who hadn't been listening.

'Conor. So unassuming.'

'Ah yes,' said Eric. 'The reluctant hero.'

Liam nodded agreement. 'Backing nervously into the limelight, as someone said.'

The girl looked at them, uncertain.

'What we mean is,' said Eric, 'he's the complete professional.'

'Always on the job,' said Liam.

Onstage, Michael was winding up.

'I think by now everyone knows who I'm talking about, so…'

The audience was already applauding.

'Ladies and gentlemen, may I present Frank Dooley and TP Muldowney, or, as they will be much better known to us all… Liam and Eric!'

Loud and affectionate applause broke out, and Conor stood to join in, as the two tottered on, bang in character, pretending bewilderment, peering myopically at the audience, smiling and nodding. Michael took an arm of each, led them downstage and pointed at Conor.

'Well, what do you think of this chap?'

'No need to shout!' shouted Eric, and got his laugh.

'I'm so sorry,' said Michael. 'I was told you were a little hard of hearing.'

'That's my character. Real life, I'm as sharp as a tack.'

Michael mumbled an apology, which Eric interrupted.

'Now, what was the question?'

'I just wondered what you thought of this chap.'

They all looked at Conor, who stood smiling at the double act he so well knew.

'He's all right,' said Eric. 'Still a little wet behind the ears.'

'But if he works hard,' said Liam, 'he'll probably make the grade.'

Eric nodded in agreement. The audience were enjoying the banter, though many of them, more used to the rustic tones of Eric and Liam on the farm, were surprised at how posh they sounded in these new surroundings.

'Actually, he's come on a lot,' said Eric. 'He's really quite generous.'

'Really? You mean he... gives you presents?'

'Oh, God, no,' said Liam. 'Never bought a drink in his life.'

'I meant on set,' said Eric. 'He lets you have your space. Never hogs things.'

Conor gave a little nod of appreciation.

'And do you see much of him outside work?'

'No, no,' said Eric. 'Couldn't afford to.'

'Not quite our class you see,' said Liam.

Eric adopted a more serious air.

'Actually,' he said, 'his private life has always been rather a mystery.'

Conor had a moment of anxiety, but no-one could have told.

Eric continued. 'I don't really believe he's had one'.

'You see,' Liam explained. 'He lived for his work, and his work was *The Days*. There was no room in his life for anything else.'

The audience applauded, and Conor, greatly relieved, looked modestly at the floor. For a moment even, he found himself wishing it was true.

6

It was after midnight, and in the Café Vangelis, Conor sat alone at his usual table watching the last group of diners taking their leave.

'Good night, now,' Rose called. 'Thanks very much.'

She closed the door behind them and hurried to the table, clearing the dishes and taking them to the hatch.

'Mam,' she said, 'could I go on?'

'Are you jokin' me?'

'Ah, Mam, please. I'll do all the cleanin' up tomorrow.'

'Promises…' said the voice behind the hatch.

'I've to meet Jason.'

'Oh, go on,' said Queenie, emerging from the kitchen, 'before I burst into tears.'

'Ah, thanks, Mam.'

Rose gave her mother a hug and disappeared into the kitchen.

Queenie went on clearing the table, watched by the

only remaining diner, Conor, as he sipped wine and pretended to study a script.

In a moment, Rose came out, miraculously transformed, pulling on a coat.

'Good night, Mam.'

'Good night, love.'

'Good night, Mr O'Hara.'

'Good night, Rose.'

As she left, Queenie pulled down a blind on the window. Turning to go back to the kitchen, she glanced over at Conor.

'Have you no home to go to?'

Conor held up the wine bottle, still half-full.

I've all this to drink,' he said.

Queenie took the remaining dishes from the table to the hatch.

'Why don't you come and help?' said Conor.

She turned and looked at him. 'Sure why not?' she said.

From inside the hatch, she grabbed a glass from somewhere, wiped it on her apron, came across and sat at his table. Conor filled his glass and hers.

'I'm Conor.'

'I know,' she said.

He looked at her quizzically.

'The girls told me. They all watch your programme.'

She had a strong Dublin accent. Southside, he thought. Ringsend maybe.

'But you don't?' he said.

She shook her head.

'Why not?'

'Amn't I workin' every night, seven nights a week, puttin' bread on the table? When would I get the time to watch telly?'

She lifted her glass, banged it on his and drank.

'The kids say you're very good, though.'

Conor looked sceptical, but said nothing.

'They do,' she said. 'They think you're the dog's bollocks.'

Conor grinned.

'That's the nicest thing anybody ever called me.'

'But do you never get fed up?' she asked. 'Like, doin' the same thing for fifteen years.'

He shrugged.

'How many years have you been cooking food?'

'Sixteen.'

'There you go. And you're very good at it.' He spooned a little sauce from the sauceboat and put it in his mouth. 'A man could kill for that.'

'I'm glad you liked it,' she said. 'Sure, don't you need buildin' up? All those women chasin' you.'

She drank from her glass, looking at him over the rim.

'I don't see you chasing me,' said Conor.

'I bloody well am,' she said. 'Chasin' you out of here.'

She put down her empty glass and stood. 'I've work to do.'

He stood up and she picked up his coat from the other chair and hustled him roughly into it. He grinned, unaccustomed to such treatment.

* * *

On stage, it was still the turn of Eric and Liam.

'Would it be fair,' asked Michael, 'to describe you two as the criminal element on Downhill Farm?'

They looked at him as if deeply offended.

Michael turned to the audience. 'Perhaps we should ask the viewer to be the judge.'

He turned to look at the monitor and the pictures came up.

EXT. YARD. DOWNHILL FARM. DAY.

Lisa walks across from the house to Liam and Eric's cottage, carrying a pile of clean laundry. She knocks on the door, opens it and looks in.

LISA

Are you decent?

INT. LIAM AND ERIC'S COTTAGE. DAY.

ERIC

You're all right, love.

Eric and Liam sit at either end of the kitchen table, doing some unexplained task with eggs, several bottles of HP sauce and French mustard. They take the eggs out of a large bowl, then, with a little brush, paint little dabs of sauce or mustard on each. Sometimes, from a little pile on the table between them, they will take a small pinch of chicken down and adhere it gently to the egg's surface.

When each egg is done, it is placed carefully in one of the many egg-boxes piled on the table. They continue with this work all through the scene.

LISA

(Coming in) I brought your laundry.

LIAM

Ah you're a little star, what are you?

LISA

A little star. *(She puts the laundry down and looks at the work going on)* What are ye doin'?

LIAM

Th'eggs.

ERIC

The free-range.

Lisa looks puzzled.

LISA

I meant to ask about that. Like, the notice on the gate. 'Free Range Eggs.'

They nod and continue working.

LISA

(Continuing) But we haven't any hens.

LIAM

Better off without hens. They can be a terrible scourge.

ERIC

And where you have hens, you have foxes.

LISA

So... *(mystified)* ... where do you get the eggs?

ERIC

Where everybody else gets them. The supermarket.

LIAM

We buy twelve dozen a week, bring them home, paint on the henshit and sell them on to our customers.

LISA

But... that's dishonest!

They break off work for a moment and stare at her.

ERIC

What do you mean, dishonest?

LIAM

How dare you!

ERIC

Those eggs cost us two pound fifty a dozen
and we sell them on for three pound fifty...

LIAM

So when you consider the trouble and
expense of goin' into the supermarket every
week... and then the artwork...

> *They resume the painting, still
> offended.*

LISA

But it's cheatin'. They're not free-range.

ERIC

(Puts down his brush) Listen, child. These
customers of ours, they're back every week,
lookin' for all they can get.

LIAM

And do you know what they tell us?
(She shakes her head)
They say that after tastin' our eggs, they
could never look at a shop egg again.

ERIC

(Nods emphatically)
So who are we cheatin'?

> *He picks up his brush with a flourish
> and in doing so knocks over an egg,
> which smashes on the floor.*

LIAM

Ah, Jaze, Eric will you mind yourself. That
sorta thing ates into the profits.

ERIC

Sure, can't we scramble it for the tea?

> *They continue working.*

* * *

As the picture faded on the screen, Michael threw out an arm.

'Ladies and gentlemen,' he called. 'The inimitable... Eric and Liam!'

There was a round of applause that Dick had no need to encourage. Frank and TP took their bows in the old theatrical way. Then they came to Conor, who stood applauding with the others, and shook his hand.

'Bless you both,' said Conor.

The applause continued as they walked slowly to their seats, beside Tony and Lance, waving in acknowledgement. Dick signalled to the audience to cool it, and Michael took centre stage.

'Now, apart from lovable old codgers,' he said, 'there is, in all everyday stories of country folk, one essential character…'

At the side of the stage, Dick put a hand to his ear, listening to a message from above. 'Arseholes,' he said quietly, and moved out of the shadows into the light of the stage, holding his arms high and crossing them slowly, an indication that all was not well.

'And that is, of course…' said Michael, before noticing Dick and breaking off.

After a brief conference, Michael stepped downstage and spoke.

'I'm sorry everybody, we're having the obligatory technical hitch. Trouble at the sound desk. It'll take about fifteen minutes to put right and in the meantime, could I ask you all to help us by staying in your seats, except for the most dire emergencies.'

The audience tittered dutifully. Those on stage stood as the researcher came on from behind and began to usher them off backstage, to what was known in the business as hospitality.

All followed, except Conor, whose instinct in these matters never failed him. He walked slowly to the steps on the side of the stage and down to the audience, where he went from one to another, shaking hands, remembering faces, thanking them for coming.

The hospitality suite was a large, comfortable room with chairs, tables and a bar. As those who had been on stage came through, they joined others already there, including some due to appear later in the show. This coming together led naturally to much greeting and kissing, and chief among those kissed and greeted was a very glamorous lady called Sylvana, who had last been seen in the role of Daphne, bride-to-be of Sir Myles. It was plain from the attention she was receiving that she had moved on to higher things since then.

As her old companions from *The Days* gathered round, the TV crew interviewing her was forced to step back, and the stills photographers from the national dailies stepped in to take their place.

Lance watched all this, but took no part. And as a tray of drinks was passing, he collected two and carried them back to Eric and Liam, in a quiet corner.

'Ah, thank you, old boy,' said Eric.

'No, no, thank *you*,' said Lance.

'What on earth for?'

'Flying the flag. Keeping the faith.' He took a long draught. 'Praising our hero.'

'I need hardly say, old boy,' said Liam, 'that the words choked us.'

Eric nodded in emphatic agreement.

'I suppose it really *is* over.'

'Looks rather like it.'

'But he did the same thing last year.'

'And the year before. Then the last-ditch change of heart.'

Lance shook his head. 'Those were just about money. Negotiations. This time he's gone public.'

'No chance of simply carrying on?'

'We thought of it, but well...' He shrugged. 'Hamlet without the prince.'

'Well, you've got the gravediggers,' said Eric.

Lance gave his bleak smile.

'We're quite prepared to grovel,' said Liam.

'Oh, I've been doing plenty of that,' said Lance. 'I've shown him all the letters, pleading with him not to go. I've even *written* some.'

Liam and Eric looked shocked.

He nodded, shamefaced. 'From women of all ages. Saying how much poorer their lives would be...'

'Actually,' said Eric, 'we worked out how it might be done. New owner moves in, complete bastard, evicts Eric and Liam, bribes several corrupt politicians and gets planning permission for enormous housing estate on the land.'

Liam took up the story. 'Meanwhile, scenes in Scotland. Family doing well but missing Downhill terribly. Aisling and Luke come to visit and carry dreadful stories back to Dermot.'

'Then, you see,' said Eric, 'we thought we'd have an

hour-long Christmas Special. Dermot suddenly shows up, finds Eric and Liam living in a tent – at the point of death. Takes on the bastard builder, exposes him and moves back to Downhill.'

'We even thought of a title,' said Liam. 'Dermot Saves the Day.'

Lance nodded sadly but said nothing.

'You might mention it to him,' said Eric.

'Oh, yes, I will,' said Lance, without conviction.

No-one spoke for a moment.

'But you don't really think there's a chance, do you?'

Lance sighed. 'A very faint one. If we can stir up sufficient public demand. He loves that. Why else,' he added casually, 'do you think we set all this up?'

He looked around the room, at Sam, gazing up into the eyes of a young film director called Kirk. At Eve and little Stephen, by the door, grabbing a moment with Dick. At Sylvana, who had resumed her TV interview. And at Linda, her eyes searching the room for Conor.

Poor soul, thought Lance. Still hoping.

He walked away, to where the cameras were.

Eric and Liam sighed and reached for a passing drinks tray. Alone among the cast, they were always referred to by their character names. Only those who had known them in the old days of the fit-ups still referred to them as Frank and TP. They had travelled the roads of Ireland with the old touring companies for thirty years before television, and there was hardly a village in Ireland where they had not been known. When the magic box arrived, it seemed that their living was gone, but then came *The Days* and they were back in harness.

It was inspired casting, not just for what they brought to the roles, but for all those in the rural parishes of Ireland, for whom they were a precious link with the past. For TP and Frank, the coming of Eric and Liam meant an unexpected extension of their working lives. But it was far more than that. They could remember coming into a town, fitting up all day, lights, tabs, scenery; setting eighty chairs and then playing to an audience of ten in a sodden tent. On *The Days*, they had their day in the sun, with audiences they could not have dreamed of.

At last, Conor appeared at the door, lingering a moment, till people turned. Which, of course, they did, raising their glasses to him. Conor smiled in acknowledgement, then spotted Sylvana. For a moment, he caught his breath, shaken. She waved to him, her eyes lighting up, and as he recovered and waved back, the TV cameraman swung around to catch him.

Sylvana stood up and put her hand on the interviewer's arm.

'I wonder, would you mind awfully,' she said. 'I haven't seen Conor in yonks.'

'Of course not,' he said. 'Perhaps later...'

She was already weaving across the room towards him, several stills photographers following in her wake. Even in this glamorous assembly she stood out.

As she came close to him, she held out her arms.

'Sylvana!' said Conor.

'Conor, darling!' She melted graciously into his embrace and the cameras clicked.

'How long is it?' she asked, although she knew to the day.

'Must be three years,' he said. 'You look wonderful.'

He glanced at the photographers, then took her arm and led her aside, behind a pillar, where they stood very close, and Sylvana gazed up at him with those well-practised, shining eyes. As they talked, quietly, they must have given to the many onlookers an impression of an intimate and loving reunion.

Conor began. 'What the hell are you doing here?' he said, pushing a stray lock of hair back from her forehead.

She smiled. 'I was invited. And, of course, I jumped at the chance.'

'You're here to make trouble, aren't you?'

Her eyes widened, as if he had suggested something shocking. 'How could you even *think*…'

He interrupted. 'Just let me get one thing straight. When you left the show…'

She interrupted. 'When you had me fired.'

'I did no such…'

She put her hand to his mouth, laughing. Already dreaming up captions, the photographers snapped the picture.

'Oh, but you *did*, darling. And I know *why* you did.'

123

He kissed her forehead. It was like an impulse he couldn't resist.

'You're going to rake up the past, then?'

'Isn't that what this programme is all about?'

'I think you know what I mean. Do you intend to talk about us?'

She smiled. 'You'd like to smash my face in, wouldn't you?'

He shook his head. 'You don't really think that.'

'Oh, but I do.' She took the button on his jacket and pulled him towards her. 'I think you're a cruel bastard,' she murmured.

His fingers touched her neck.

'Matter of fact,' he said. 'I've never raised my hand to a living soul.'

'You never needed to. You had other ways of being cruel. You could manipulate people, discard them, get them fired... You had the power.'

'I think you overestimate me, darling.'

'I wonder sometimes what you would do *without* that power. What if you wanted to punish someone you had no power to hurt, someone who didn't need you?'

'You mean – someone like you?'

'Yes.' She looked up into his eyes. 'You know, if there weren't a hundred people watching us now, I think you'd probably kill me.'

He shook his head slowly, still smiling for the cameras.

'No', he said. 'You see, I'd have to care.'

For a moment, Sylvana was uncertain. Then she recovered.

'I believe I'm on next,' she said quickly, and kissed his cheek.

As she turned away, the photographers followed, calling her name. She stopped, fell into an instant pose. The flashes went off and she moved away again.

Conor remembered that walk. And even at such a remove – three years, was it? – it still did something to him.

From her first day on set, she had made it plain that she wanted him. It was as if she believed that to be a credible seductress like Daphne, she must grow into it as Sylvana. When they rehearsed, she would find a way of touching him, whether the scene called for it or not. And when they spoke together off set, she would never stand by his side, but always directly facing him, touching, her head falling forward on his chest when she laughed.

And Conor was ready. His time in Spain with Linda had been good at first, and he had enjoyed the luxury. But he was unused to idleness, and within days he was longing to be home. Linda was in Spain all the time now and he was not particularly missing her. He had the feeling that this, his longest affair, had run its course.

And now this exotic creature was throwing herself at his feet. She would worry about her character and ask his advice, wishing often that they could have more time together, away from the set. He knew what this meant, but he was in no hurry to invite her to the flat. Not yet.

But when he felt the time was ripe...

7

It was a brilliant night, full of stars. Staging by Conor O'Hara. He had turned the lights down in his apartment and Sylvana, underlit by the streetlights, stood by the window, looking down at the river.

Conor came with two glasses of wine and handed one to her.

'Welcome to Downhill Farm,' he said.

He would have clinked glasses, but they were the good ones, the Baccarat.

'Thank you,' said Sylvana, and drank.

'Do you think they're happy with me?

'*I'm* happy,' said Conor.

'And Lance?'

'Lance has never been happy. He's made it his life's work to be miserable.'

He led her to the sofa.

'You see,' he went on, 'you've got something very rare in this business.'

'Have I?'

'You're playing a high-born lady,' he said, and she nodded, hanging on his words.

'Now, most actresses playing high-born ladies just do it the way other actresses have always done it. Maybe they get out a few old Jane Austen tapes and copy the voices, but that's as far as they go.

'Well, of course, you've got the voice already, but you've got so much more. You have the...' He searched for the word. '... the air. It's in-built. You *are* a high-born lady. You're perfect.'

She twined her arms around his neck. 'It's good to hear you say that. And it's so good to have someone like you to... well, to keep me right.'

He kissed her. Decorously at first, then with a little more heat. He moved to her ears and kissed her lobes gently.

'Why don't we go next door?' he whispered.

'Are you claiming your *droit du seigneur*?'

He didn't answer, and she went on: 'It's the right of a feudal lord to bed the bride of his vassal...'

He interrupted her. 'I know what it means.' And smiled, to show he was a good sport. 'But it doesn't really apply here does it? *You're* the feudal lady. I'm the vassal.'

They kissed again.

'Tell me,' said Conor. 'Where did you find that wonderful name, Sylvana? It can't be real...'

She said nothing.

'Go on. What's your real name?'

'Promise you won't tell?'

He crossed his heart.

'It's Sybil.'

He thought about it for a moment. 'Well, it's not so bad,' he said. 'You can go back to it when they make you a Dame.'

She smiled and finished her wine. Taking this as a signal, he moved closer and kissed her again. She responded, and he pulled her towards him. She stayed with him for a moment, then very gently broke away.

'No, Conor,' she said. There was a note of uncertainty. 'It's not that I don't want to. In fact, if you want the truth, there's nothing I'd like more. But… it's just too soon.'

'It's all right,' he said. 'I understand.'

He turned away and picked up his wine.

'Are you angry with me?' She seemed anxious.

'Of course not. You mustn't ever do anything you don't want to.'

'But I *do*.'

He stopped her by planting a very brotherly kiss on her lips.

'Perhaps I ought to go,' she said. 'Early start.'

'Come on,' he said. 'I'll get you a cab.'

'No, don't. I'll get the porter to call one.'

'It's no trouble.'

'And there's no need. Think of your reputation.'

He laughed at that, then picked up her coat and started to help her into it.

'Promise to ask me again?'

'You're very forward,' said Conor.

'I was a spoiled child.'

'All right, I promise.'

She leaned forward quickly and kissed him, breaking off just as quickly. 'Good night, Conor.'

'Good night, Sybil.'

She made a face and opened the door.

'See you tomorrow,' said Conor.

She nodded and slipped out. As the door closed behind her, he went and stood by the window, waiting to see her emerge, wondering if she would look up. He couldn't escape the feeling that he had been in a contest. And that he had lost.

* * *

In the hospitality suite, the noise had swelled greatly since the arrival of the actors, and Dick had to call several times for a hearing.

'Please,' he called, adding, 'for fuck's sake,' under his breath. 'Can I have your attention *please*! Bitta hush. We're ready to go again. So if you'd all take your places back on stage… Places, please.'

There was a great draining of glasses as the guests moved to the exit. Conscious of the importance of making the final entrance, Conor hung back.

As he went through the door, he looked back to where Sylvana sat, awaiting her call.

She smiled at him. 'See you soon,' she called. And blew him a kiss.

Back in the theatre, cameras and sound were in position and the onstage guests were taking their seats, as Dick walked to the edge of the stage and raised his arms for quiet.

'Thank you all for your patience,' he said. 'We're ready to go again. Now, before we were interrupted, you were applauding Eric and Liam as they took their seats. Do you mind giving us a little more of that?'

He began clapping, and the audience dutifully joined in. Then, on the signal, they brought it down and Michael stepped forward.

'Now, apart from crafty old codgers, there is, in all "everyday stories of country folk", one utterly essential character – and that is the lady of the manor, with her passion for the pleasures of the chase. Would you please welcome the internationally acclaimed star of the Oscar-winning film *Where the Wind Cries* – the lovely Sylvana O'Brien!'

Dick went into action and the applause broke out. Sylvana waited the normal three seconds, to get them all looking, then moved into the light of the entrance, paused another second, then the final stretch, to tumultuous applause. Conor too was on his feet, applauding warmly, and Sylvana walked straight to him, kissing him with

131

unmistakeable warmth. Then back to Michael and a more formal offer of the cheek.

'Sylvana,' said Michael, 'your name is now, of course, a household word…'

'Like dripping,' said Sylvana.

Michael smiled. 'Actually,' he said, 'it would be hard to think of anything less like dripping. What I'm trying to say is that, though you're known internationally through your films, it all began on *The Days*, did it not?'

'But of course. And I'll always be grateful. I couldn't have had a better beginning.'

Michael nodded at Conor. 'And what do you think of this fella?'

She looked at Conor, her head on one side, as if weighing up her answer. Conor sat smiling, waiting, wondering what might come.

'I'm trying to think how to do him justice,' she said. 'He taught me so much. And I don't agree that he had no life outside his work. He's a very private person, but he has so many sides to him.'

'Such as?'

'He loves *people*. Being *close* to people. Always good humoured, always stimulating. Always *giving*. I have such memories.'

And Conor remembered too…

They were in his apartment again. Almost half past midnight, on the sofa.

This time, though, they were working, going through scripts, hearing each other's lines. Suddenly, Sylvana threw her script down and sat back.

'Oh, bugger!' she said. 'I just hate the whole scene!'

'I think it can work.'

She talked over him, cross. 'I keep talking *down* to people. Like a stuck-up bitch. And I don't think Daphne *is* a stuck-up bitch, do you?'

He opened his mouth to reply, but she went on.

'Up to now she's been a sort of... Scarlett O'Hara with breeding.'

'Exactly what she should be, but that's not what's coming across.'

'What else can I do, with these lines?'

'Look, you really fancy Dermot and he doesn't see it, which annoys the hell out of you. So you get all snooty, you talk down to him. "Look, you fucking peasant, you're not in my league." That's what you're saying, but the reason you're *saying* it is, you're hurting like hell.'

She nodded.

'Only you've got to *show* that. Like Scarlett. All you're showing is anger, so you come across, like you say, as a stuck-up bitch.'

'But I'm *not*,' said Sylvana, like a six year old.

'Sybil!' he said loudly.

She hit him with her elbow. 'Don't ever call me that!'

133

'I'll call you a lot worse, if you don't listen. Now, read my lips. *Vulnerability*. That's the key. A little catch in the voice. Turn away. Don't let him see you're hurting. But make bloody sure the viewer sees.'

Sylvana nodded, as if seeing the light.

'Yes. But will Lance let me?'

'Bugger Lance. I'll talk to him.'

She looked at the script again. 'And that last line, "I'll send my steward over." Who, in this day and age…?'

'Yeah, it's terrible.'

He scanned a few more lines of script and shook his head. 'This writer has to go,' he said, below his breath.

She put her arms around him and kissed his ear. 'What would I do without you?'

He picked up the bottle on the table and poured, but only half a glass came out.

'Don't move,' he said, and went to the kitchen.

Sylvana took a quick look at her watch – 12.35am. She walked to the window, opened the curtains and looked out at the traffic on the quays.

'I never saw such traffic,' she said to Conor, as he came back in with a new bottle, already opened. As he filled their two glasses, she kissed his eyes and nose and ran her fingers through his hair. He put the bottle down, pulled her close and kissed her. For the first time, she allowed her body to mould with his and Conor, normally a good judge of these things, slipped a hand under her arm and began to move her towards the bedroom door. But it was no more than a step, then she stopped, still holding him, a distance between them.

'What's up?' he asked.

'I'm being vulnerable,' she said.

And Conor smiled. 'There's a time and a place…'

He moved close to her again.

'Do you really think we should?'

'Don't *you*?' he asked, as calmly as he could manage.

She hesitated, then came towards him again. At that moment the doorbell rang. 'Oh, Lord,' she said.

'Ignore it.'

'It's my taxi.'

He looked puzzled.

'I ordered it for one o'clock,' she said. 'He's come early.'

Conor was irritated, but was careful not to show it. He went to the door.

'I'll send him away.'

'No,' she said quickly. 'I mean, you know what it's like, trying to find a taxi at this hour.'

'You don't have to. You can stay.'

'I can't. I have an early start. Seven-thirty at the farm.'

'So have I, it's our scene – remember? We can go together. I'll drive you.'

The bell rang again.

'Conor, I'd love to, but we can't…'

'Can't what?'

'Arrive together. We don't want people to know, do we?'

He hesitated. But he stayed cool.

'Yes, I suppose you're right,' he said. 'Have to be discreet.'

She grabbed her coat, kissed his cheek and made for the door.

'Sorry, darling. But there'll be other times.'

As she ran out, the bell rang again. Conor's smile faded as he walked to the window and looked down to where the taxi waited.

He knew, of course, what had been happening, but he couldn't believe it. He remembered from schooldays, on Monday mornings, the lads in sixth year talking about their weekend adventures. Bragging mostly, but now and then a chilling story of a girl who promised but wouldn't deliver. They had a name for them.

But it had never happened to *him*. Never. Favours such as these had always been, so to speak, in his gift. Worst of all was the realisation that she must have planned it that way. Every move, from the beginning.

He watched as Sylvana appeared below and climbed into the taxi.

She looked crossly at the driver.

'You were supposed to be here at twelve. Where the hell were you?'

'Sorry, love,' he said, starting the car. 'It's all happenin' this evenin'.'

And as he drove away, he added, 'Excuse me for askin', but are you the one off the telly?'

Conor turned away from the window. He glanced at his watch, hesitated, then went to the cloakroom, grabbed his coat, switched off the light and left the apartment.

He walked up the quay, listening to the shouts of the revellers just a few streets away, in Temple Bar. Coming to a corner, he stopped for a moment, then turned and walked up the street, away from the river. It was an impulse, rather than a plan. And in a moment he was standing outside the Café Vangelis.

The lights in the restaurant were off and the blind on the door was down, but he could see the light from the kitchen.

He rapped on the door and waited. Nothing happened, and he was about to knock again when the door was pulled open, just the few inches allowed by the chain.

'Who's there?' said Queenie.

Before he could answer, she recognised him.

'Conor is it?'

She released the catch, grabbed his arm, looked up and down the street and pulled him inside.

'What in the name of Jesus are you doin' at this hour?'

'I saw the light,' he said lamely, looking in some shock at the shotgun she carried in her other hand.

'I hope you're not lookin' for grub,' she said, putting the gun on a table and re-locking the door.

'No, no.' He nodded at the gun. 'What's that about?'

'Oh, I've had a few late-night callers lately. Lookin' for the night's takin's. You're lucky you're still alive.'

As they talked, she was putting chairs up on the tables. He started to help her.

'Are you on your own?' he asked.

'Yeah. Listen, if it's not grub, what *are* you lookin' for?'

'Oh, I don't know. Glass of wine. Sound of a human voice...'

She looked at him, eyebrows raised.

'Well, it beats sitting in the flat, looking at the wall,' he said.

'Is this th'artistic temperament?'

Conor laughed. 'Must be. Look, I'm only round the corner. Why don't you come back... have a nightcap?'

She had finished the chairs and stood in front of him, looking up. He had forgotten how small she was.

'Do you know,' she said, 'I'm on me feet since seven this morning. The only place I'm goin' is to me bed.'

He looked at her appraisingly. She was pretty. Nice figure. Her hair was a mess, thick and black, with not a sign of grey. And she smelt of fish and garlic and God knows what. But she was pretty.

'But that doesn't mean,' she went on, 'that we can't have a drink. Only not here.'

'Where, then?'

'My place.'

'Where's that?'

'I'm in the flat upstairs.' She grabbed a bottle from the rack. 'Are you comin'?'

She headed for the kitchen and Conor followed.

'But you're not stayin' long, because I'm wrecked. Fit for nuthin'.'

The lights in the kitchen went out and he heard her climbing the narrow stairs beyond.

'Mind yourself,' she shouted.

In the days that followed, he found it difficult to remember the exact sequence of events. The flat was chaotic but filled with colour. Purples and reds. She had handed him the bottle and a corkscrew and headed for the shower. Ten minutes later she was back, in a silk robe. And slippers made to look like polar bears with yawning jaws.

He remembered her leaning across him to take her drink, her hair long, straight and shining, her skin smelling of flowers. Everything else was blurred. Whether the second bottle was opened before or after they went to the bedroom he couldn't remember. Or who made the first move. Or why, afterwards, his outer clothing was in the bedroom and his underclothing in the room outside. How was that possible?

The main event he remembered only for the image that had somehow stayed in his mind, of dolphins at play. The first clear moment of recall was of the peace that descended when it was over, when, amid small contented noises, a bedside lamp was switched on and Queenie's

139

head came up from under a sheet, her hair over her face like a tassel, but otherwise looking happy. She half-sat up on the pillow and reached for her wine. Conor lay back beside her, his pillow on the floor.

She looked down at him. 'You're terrible randy aren't you?'

'Will you look who's talking?' said Conor, as she sipped her wine. 'I thought you said you were fit for nothing.'

She looked at her empty glass. 'Is there any wine in that bottle?'

Conor stretched his arm to the bedside table, and as he picked up the bottle, knocked over a little framed colour photograph. He picked it up and looked at it. It was a picture of a small, laughing, dark-haired man.

'Who is he?'

'Me husband. Vangelis.'

'As in…?' He pointed downstairs, to the café.

She nodded. 'Though mind you, he's never seen the place.'

She reached over to her own bedside cabinet, took another, bigger picture in a white cover and showed it to Conor.

'This was at the wedding.'

It was of the same man, now with a much younger Queenie, both in elaborate Greek wedding costume, and dancing. Vangelis had a handkerchief in one hand and one leg high in the air. Conor took the picture and studied it.

'Where is he now?'

'God knows. I met him out in Greece. I was on me holidays and he was workin' in this taverna. And when the time came to go home I stayed on. He was engaged to this Greek girl but he married *me*. His family was ragin'.'

She looked at the picture.

'Hasn't he lovely little feet?' she said.

'And you lived in Greece?'

She nodded, still looking at the picture. 'T'ree years. Learned Greek an' all.'

She put the picture carefully back on the cabinet.

'He spent the summers in the village. Then, in October, when the tourists were gone, he'd go off workin' on the ships.'

'Must have been lonely for you.'

'Yeah, well, I'd go home for the Christmas and stay on. Then back out again at Easter and wait for him. And then one year, must be ten year ago now, I was out there, waitin' and waitin', and he never came.'

'And you haven't seen him since?'

'Well, he's turned up now and again. Like as if nothin' had happened. The bad penny. And I get th'odd letter, maybe once a year. But I don't think he'll ever really settle. Like, it wouldn't be his way.'

'He should be hung.'

'Oh, sure hangin's too good for him. It's a good kick in th'arse he wants.'

He laughed and she laughed with him.

'He was nice all the same. He just shouldn't ever have got married.'

Conor looked again at the little picture.

'So he's Rose's father?'

'And Maria's,' said Queenie. 'She's still at school,' she added, before Conor could ask.

'And then you have the two sisters?'

'Three. Two here, one at the caterin' college.'

'It's amazing.'

'Ah, you get used to it,'

'No, I mean,' said Conor, 'it's just like Dermot.'

'Who?'

Conor grinned. 'Oh, I forgot, you never watch. He's my character. The one I play on TV. He was left in his twenties to bring up his brothers and sisters. Only difference is, mine's make-believe. You really do it. I think you're marvellous.'

'I'm a feckin' wonder.'

'But you *are*. And you're so... upfront about everything. You say what you mean. I'm not used to that. In my business, no-one does it. It's dog eat dog.'

Queenie yawned. 'Look, would you ever stop talkin' and pour the shaggin' wine?'

Conor grinned and reached for the bottle.

8

Tony sat at his wide, pristine desk, rolling a pencil between his fingers. Conor sat opposite. Lance stood at the window, doing his best not to be involved.

'I'm sorry, Tony,' said Conor. 'I think she has to go.'

'Oh, for Christ's sake,' said Tony, but Conor kept going.

'I'm as fond of her as you are. And she's a joy to work with. I'm just not happy with the character, she's not working.'

'What the hell do you mean?'

'She's playing a tough, ruthless opportunist intent on getting her way, whatever the cost. But she keeps playing *against* that, looking for sympathy.'

He looked over at Lance. 'You must have seen that, Lance.'

'Of course I have,' said Lance. 'I think it's rather good, shows she's vulnerable, bit of depth...'

'Exactly,' said Tony.

He did his trick of breaking the pencil, throwing the bits on the desk, getting up, walking to the window and talking with his back turned.

'The response to her has been terrific, they love her.'

'Balls,' said Conor.

'And she has a wonderful arse.'

'I'll grant you the arse,' said Conor. 'The arse works. The personality doesn't.'

Tony turned, came back, sat down noisily, sighed, leaned back, looked at the ceiling, sighed again.

'Lance?' he said. It was his way of asking Lance to give his view.

'I think she's great in the show,' said Lance. 'But perhaps we *ought* to be thinking of ways to write her out.' He added, by way of afterthought, 'Since we'll probably be losing her anyway.'

Conor looked up sharply.

'Why do you say that?'

'New feature film. She's up for the lead.'

Conor grinned. 'Oh come on, Lance. How many times have you heard that?'

'They've been on to me about availability,' said Tony.

'What's the film?'

'Oh, what is it now? *Where the Wind Cries*. Something like that. Budget's twenty million.'

'She's got no chance.'

'Who knows? They've called her back.'

'She'll fall on her face. She just doesn't have it.' He thought a moment. 'Tell her tomorrow, okay?'

'Tell her what?' said Tony.

Conor held a thumb down. 'Tomorrow,' he said.

'How in God's name can we? We don't even have a story.'

'The story's not a problem. Riding accident.'

Tony stared at him.

Conor spelled it out. 'Something spooks the horse, he heads for a wall. Remote camera in the ditch, the horse takes off, low-angle shot of the horse's balls, legs in all directions. Freeze the frame, perfect cliffhanger. Think of the irony.'

They looked blank.

Conor spoke patiently. 'It was her whole life!'

He traced a headline in the air with his hand.

'She died as she lived. In the saddle.'

There was a short silence.

'What do *you* say Lance?' said Tony

Lance yawned. 'Oh, I can just… picture it all,' he said.

'Then next week,' said Conor, warming to the story, 'open with a close-up, pale face, staring eyes, little trickle of blood on the corner of her lips. Then the matching shot of the horse, lying across her, the froth on his lips flecked with blood. That'll work.'

'You mean… the horse dies too?'

'Oh I think so,' said Conor. 'Not in reality, of course, that would be cruel. We can't have cruelty to horses.'

'God no,' said Tony, 'not to horses.'

'You'll tell her then? Tomorrow?'

'For God's sake why tomorrow? What's the rush?'

'Because if she gets this film, which I still can't believe, she can say she walked out on me. I won't have that.'

He turned to go. As he reached the door, Tony called him.

'Conor.'

He turned.

'She wouldn't be walking out on *you*. She'd be walking out on the *show*.'

Conor looked puzzled. 'What's the difference?' he said.

When he had gone, there was a moment's silence, before Lance spoke.

'Are you going to do it?'

'Well, as you said, we'll probably lose her anyway.'

'So we'll be the villains again. And Conor will be the hero who tried to save her.'

'Yes. Little interviews in the Sundays. Deeply upset.'

Lance nodded. '"I was on the point of walking out," declares angry soap star.'

'Hm... but this time,' said Tony, 'I'd rather like Sylvana to discover the truth. I mean, if someone could tell her. In the strictest confidence.'

Lance sighed. 'I wonder who,' he murmured.

* * *

Conor was glad he had discovered the Café Vangelis. He had got into the habit of eating there and, if Queenie took the notion, staying on.

Tonight, the few customers who had been in had left early. Queenie had locked the door smartly, grabbed a bottle and showed it to him for approval, saying nothing.

'Put that on my bill,' he said.

'Don't think I won't,' she called back over her shoulder, as she climbed the stairs.

Now they were in her sitting room, the red and purple one. Like a hoor's parlour, as Queenie put it. She sat at one end of the vast, voluptuous couch, drinking her wine, while Conor lay full length on the deep cushions, his head on her lap.

'I believe it's just like real life,' she said.

'What is?'

'Your show.'

He shook his head. 'No.'

'Well that's what Rose says.'

'*Real* life is unpredictable,' he said. '*Real* people don't know what's in store for them... It's outside their control. But you see, *we* know what's coming. When people watch soaps, they pretend to themselves that we're real, but deep down they know we're not. They know that everything we do is planned, it's in the script. There's writers and directors pulling the strings.

'And that's a great comfort to people, knowing that

even if *they* don't know what's coming around the corner, all *our* problems are kind of… under control.'

Queenie looked down to see if he'd finished.

'Aren't people very thick?' she said.

Conor laughed.

'I suppose they are, thank God.' He sat up and put an arm round her. 'That's what I love about you,' he said.

'What is?'

'The way you come out with things. No pretence.'

'Ah, I'd be no good at that,' she said. 'Not like you.'

He looked at her sharply.

'Actin' I mean,' she said.

'Oh, I see what you mean,' he said. He looked relieved.

'Isn't that all it is? Pretendin'?'

'Well it's a *bit* more than that. When you take on a role, a new character, it's like putting on his clothes. Later, you're putting on his skin.'

She made a face.

'But you're right,' he said. 'That's what it is. Pretending. We pretend for a living, don't we?'

He said it as if it had just occurred to him. He leaned over to kiss her, but she slipped deftly under his arms, stood up and picked up the bottle.

'I don't know about *you*,' she said. 'But I'm goin' to bed.'

She walked into the bedroom, leaving the door open. Conor grinned and followed.

* * *

Michael walked across the stage to where Lance sat.

'Lance O'Leary,' he said, 'longtime director of *The Days of Downhill Farm*, you must know this man better than most?'

Lance inclined his head, denying nothing.

'What's he like? Big head? Suspect temperament?'

'Well, we never actually came to blows,' said Lance.

'I wouldn't hit a man with glasses,' Conor called from across the stage.

'I suppose he's been known to throw the odd wobbly,' said Lance. 'Which of us hasn't? But it was always because he cared. And never for himself. It was always for the show, and the people in the show.'

In the seat beside him, Tony nodded.

'Everything else – all the little simple pleasures – took a back seat.'

* * *

Standing on one leg, Conor expertly slipped the other one into the trouser-leg and pulled the full garment up to his 34-inch waist.

Queenie was sitting up in bed, reading a cookery book. *The Naked Chef.*

'And another thing about *real* life,' said Conor, who had been talking for some time. 'It's so unfair. In the *real* world, bad guys, if they're smart, do very well. Good guys get their asses kicked. It's not like that in soaps.'

'Is it not?' said Queenie, only half-listening.

He shook his head.

'In soapland, people always get their just desserts. Their past catches up. They get what's coming to them. And they're consistent too, I mean they always stay true to type. You can *depend* on them. In real life, you can depend on nobody.'

He knotted his tie carefully, at the dressing-table mirror, and came and sat on the bed.

'And it's important to people, I think, to have something constant in their lives, even if it's only on the telly.'

'Jaze, will you stop,' said Queenie. 'Sure isn't it only a play?'

'That's how it started! But it became part of people's lives. And you can't mess about with people's lives.'

She looked up from her book and put her hand to his face.

'You shouldn't take it so serious,' she said.

'But it's true. People care about us. They come back from their holidays and the first question they ask is "What's been happenin' to the Days?"'

She went back to her book.

'Haven't they little to worry them?'

'You see, Queenie, people in real life don't know who they can trust, who among their nearest and dearest is going to stab them in the back. But they know they can always rely on old Dermot Day to do the decent thing.'

Queenie looked at him surreptitiously over her book.

150

She had become fond of him, but sometimes she wondered if perhaps he was a little bit crazy.

'And that's not a bad thing for people,' he went on, 'to have someone in their lives they can trust.'

He looked at himself in the mirror.

* * *

Michael's instincts were telling him that Lance and Tony, however worthy, were not compelling. In the audience, the coughing had started. In the sitting rooms, they'd be checking the other channels.

'Well, Sylvana,' he said, crossing the stage, 'I know you're up to your eyes in your new film and we're really grateful to you for finding time to join us tonight.'

'I wouldn't have missed it for the world,' she said, squeezing Conor's hand, telling him how she would hate parting.

'You're flying out first thing tomorrow. Bali, I believe?'

She nodded. A slightly jaded smile that said what a bore it was.

'Film going well, I hope.'

'One never knows, does one?'

'Well, no,' said Michael. 'I suppose one doesn't. But before I let you go... We've already shown your *first* appearance on *The Days*. Now I'd like to show one of your last.'

He turned and pointed to the screen.

'Have a look.'

151

EXT. DOWNHILL FARM. DAY.

The farmyard. Open on the slurry tank, near which the truck and a muckspreader are standing. Peter comes from the barn with a box of apples, which he puts on the back of the truck, the last of the load. As he puts up the tailgate, Dermot and Lisa come from the house. Dermot calls Peter's name.

PETER

Yeah?

DERMOT

I'm taking Lisa today. You don't mind staying back?

PETER

No. Why?

DERMOT

We need to spread slurry on the hill field.

PETER

Today?

DERMOT

There's a change forecast. Has to be today.

PETER

But that's a job for Eric and Liam.

DERMOT

(Shakes his head) Eric's got a bug. And Liam
can't manage the spreader. So you're
elected.

> *He takes a pair of heavy gloves from*
> *the cab of the truck and throws them*
> *to him.*

DERMOT

(Continuing) Use these. Keep your hands
clean.

> *Peter catches them, but he is not*
> *happy. As Dermot and Lisa turn back*
> *towards the house, Dermot gives her*
> *the ghost of a wink. She looks at him*
> *reprovingly and goes into the house.*

PETER (O.S.)

Hey! *(Dermot turns. Peter nods his head*
towards the gate, says quietly) Royal visit.

Dermot looks. (His POV) Daphne, Lady Tregorran, is riding into the yard on her magnificent horse, looking rather magnificent herself. Luke comes out of the barn as she dismounts. Barely looking at him, she hands him the reins and walks across to Dermot.

DAPHNE

Good morning, Dermot.

DERMOT

Morning, Lady Tregorran.

DAPHNE

(Corrects him) Daphne.

DERMOT

(Nods in acknowledgement) To what do we owe the pleasure?

DAPHNE

Oh, same old thing.

DERMOT

The hunt?

DAPHNE

Now, Dermot, before you get all cross, just
listen.

> *She takes his arm and walks away*
> *across the yard with him, watched by*
> *Peter and Luke, who are pretending*
> *to work at the muckspreader; and,*
> *from behind a curtain in the house,*
> *Lisa.*

DAPHNE

(Continuing) You see, it's the first hunt of
the season Saturday week and I so want it to
go well. Now it's not your entire farm we're
talking about, it's that one little strip,
between the river and the spinney. It's well
away from your other land and...

DERMOT

(Interrupts) I'm sorry, Lady Tregorran...

DAPHNE

Daphne.

DERMOT

Daphne. I'm sorry, but we've been over all
this. I don't want the hunt anywhere near my
land.

DAPHNE

(Interrupts) But that's not what I'm asking. I
have a new proposal. I thought – or rather
we thought, the hunt, I mean – that since
that field is so vital to the hunt, and since
you don't use it for anything, you might be
interested in selling.

*Dermot opens his mouth but finds no
words.*

DAPHNE

(Continuing) And we're prepared to make a
very generous offer.

DERMOT

(Interrupts) I'm sorry, it's just not for sale.
(A beat) And actually, I do have plans for
that field. We're going to plough it and… put
in a crop.

Shot of Peter, looking surprised.

DAPHNE

What kind of crop?

DERMOT

(After a brief hesitation) Lavender.

DAPHNE

(A sudden smile) Oh, how lovely! May I come and walk through it when it's in bloom?

DERMOT

You'll be very welcome. *(Nods at the horse)* But not him.

He smiles at her and she smiles back.

DAPHNE

(Rueful) Well I suppose that's that. *(She comes closer to him, looking up into his eyes.)* The most important thing is... that we shouldn't fall out.

DERMOT

No reason why we should. *(A beat)* Though
mind you, I wouldn't say we had a great deal
in common, you and I.

DAPHNE

Oh, I don't know. I'm sure we'd find lots of
things we could agree on. Given time... *(She
comes closer. Fingers his waistcoat buttons.)*
Why don't you could come over to the house
one evening? Myles tends to retire early.

DERMOT

We'd like that.

> *She is very conscious that he has said
> 'we,' not 'I'.*

How is Sir Myles?

DAPHNE

I'm afraid he's a little off colour. He has to
be careful, you see, not to strain himself.
But he will keep trying, poor darling.

> *Dermot nods in understanding. She
> looks past him, smiles and gives a
> little wave. Lisa, standing in the*

doorway of the house, with Baby Stephen in her arms, smiles uncertainly back.

DAPHNE

(Continuing) Your wife? *(He nods)* Sweet...

She turns away, takes the reins of the horse from Luke, smiles graciously at him and mounts the horse.

She rides out of the yard without looking back.

Dermot watches her go, not totally unaffected by her.

PETER

(Incredulous) Lavender?

* * *

As the scene faded to black, and the audience applauded, Sylvana inclined her head and smiled in acknowledgement.

'Watching it again,' said Michael, 'and you must forgive me if I seem nosey, but was all that just acting?'

Conor and Sylvana looked at each other as if

159

nonplussed. Overacting a bit, but the audience giggled, loving it. Michael pressed for an answer.

'Any… chemistry there?'

Sylvana hesitated. Conor smiled, hiding his anxiety.

'I'm sorry to disappoint you, Michael,' said Sylvana. 'We were very good pals, of course, but there was no romance.'

She said it as if she rather regretted there wasn't, and hesitated before going on.

'I suppose if there had been, I could have made a fortune, writing my memoirs. Having them serialised in the Sunday papers.' She squeezed Conor's hand. 'I suppose I still could.'

She smiled roguishly at Conor, but he knew what she was saying.

'You were just a year in the show,' said Michael, 'before tragedy struck.'

She gave a little comic sniff, as if choking back a tear.

Michael took up the mood, lowering his voice to a hush.

'You never did get to walk through his lavender, did you?'

She shook her head sadly.

'Were you sorry to leave?'

'Oh, yes. It had been such a happy time. But when the film offer came up…'

'*Where the Wind Cries*,' said Michael.

'Yes, well, I really had no choice. And they were very good about letting me go.'

She looked over at Tony and Lance, who sat modest and inscrutable.

'They picked a rather... er... gruesome way to kill you off, didn't they?'

'Yes. Didn't they?'

As the sound of galloping hooves came up, loud and echoing, they turned to look at the screen. All around the auditorium the speakers boomed and trembled, then a distant hunting horn sounded against the baying of the hounds until finally the horses came into view, riding in full cry across the field, towards a high dike.

Sylvana rode near the front, as always, but as the leading horses rose, one of them swerved into her path. There was a scream, as the camera in the ditch took over, with its frightening picture of horse and rider, seen from below, the horse's legs spread widely, its chest and belly coming down. Then Sylvana flying sideways, falling in the ditch, looking up and screaming as the shadow of the falling horse came closer. And as her arms came up to cover her eyes, they froze the frame.

In the theatre, the audience were half-applauding, half-laughing. You could never tell with audiences.

'Some exit!' said Michael.

Sylvana grimaced. 'I did think they might have come up with something a little more original.'

'But it was… quick and merciful.'

'Hm.' She hesitated. 'One thing I *would* like to say…'

Conor held his breath.

'Any success I've enjoyed, since my days with the Days, I owe to Conor, and the many, many lessons he taught me.'

She leaned across and kissed him.

'Bless you, darling,' said Conor.

She stood, to loud applause, kissed Michael's cheek, gave a little curtsey to the audience and walked, with that characteristic raised chin, to the exit.

9

Michael joined in the applause, then turned back to his star guest.

'So what now, Conor? Any plans?'

'I'd like to think I'd go on working. Acting is all I know, and an actor's job is to play all the parts he can. For the last fifteen years I've played only one. I suppose I'd like to find out if I can play anything else.'

He looked around and spoke to the audience.

'So if anyone out there has work to offer, I'm available.'

They smiled back, loving his modesty.

'But for the moment,' he went on, 'I intend to take a little time off. Live in my own skin for a while. Several people have said that, up to now, I've had no life outside the show. Maybe now it's time to put that right.'

'Marry and settle down?' said Michael. 'Grow roses?'

'Possibly. Though I've had fifteen years of growing things. But there are lots of things I used to enjoy, things I can go back to.'

* * *

He was in the familiar sleigh-bed in the room above the café, her nails in his back, little cries coming from her.

And when it was over, he lay still, looking down at her.

'You're wonderful,' he said.

'Yeah, I know,' said Queenie.

'I think you're probably the only real person I know.'

She had never been comfortable with talk like that.

'You mean,' she said, 'you've got one of those rubber women at home, the ones you blow up?'

He grinned and shook his head. 'I mean, I think I'm in love with you.'

'Will you stop!' she said. 'You just like your oats.'

She put an arm round his neck and tried to pull him down but he resisted.

'No, listen. I've never said that to anybody before. Except on camera.'

'Chancer.'

'It's true.'

'Sure you've had thousands of women.'

He shrugged. 'Some.'

'All the glamour queens.'

'Well, maybe that's it.'

'What's it?'

'None of them were real. Like I said, you're the first real person I've been with.'

'Oh, Jaze, I'm real all right. And I've the stretchmarks to prove it.'

She looked up at him, appraisingly.

164

'What's up?' he asked.

'I was just wonderin'. If they could see you now, what would they think?'

'What would who think?'

'The ones out there. The viewers.'

He grinned. 'They'd be dead jealous.'

'I'd say they'd be very annoyed, very let down. The big hero, rollin' around in his pelt.'

He grinned, turned away and lay back, looking at the ceiling.

'They're going to miss us.'

'Who are?'

'The ones out there.'

She looked at him, wondering what he meant.

'We're finishing in June,' he told her.

'But don't you finish every June? And then you're back in September, like the black-and-white geese in Booterstown.'

He shook his head. 'Not this year. We're gone for good.'

Queenie arched her eyebrows. 'But why? Isn't it very popular? Numero uno?'

He nodded.

'So why would they take it off?'

'Well, it wasn't exactly their decision. I told them I was leaving.'

He gave a little grimace, to show what a tough decision it had been.

'But you mustn't say, even to Rose. I only told them yesterday. It hasn't been announced yet.'

She was quiet for a moment, then a thought struck her.

'Jaze, I could ring up the *News of the World*, make meself a few pound.'

He opened his mouth to speak but she spoke across him.

'Only coddin'.'

She stretched across him, took his glass of wine and drank it.

'What did they say?' she asked. 'When you told them.'

'Oh, they were very good about it. I think perhaps they were expecting it.'

As it happened, they weren't.

* * *

'What the fuck do you mean?' said Tony, snapping his pencil.

'It's simple enough,' said Conor. 'I'm not renewing.'

'Look,' said Lance. 'Why don't we discuss this in a civilised way?'

'What's to discuss? I'm simply giving you notice, as I'm obliged to do.'

'You're walking out on the show! Pulling the plug!'

Conor shrugged. 'I reckon I've given it enough. You've had your money's worth.'

Lance moved to the window, enabling Tony to carry the flag.

'What about the people you're putting out of work? Or do you give a shit?'

'Oh, you'll be all right, Tony. Permanent staff. Little move to religious programmes, suit you down to the ground.'

'Don't be such a smart bastard! What about the cast? Don't they mean anything?'

'Not an awful lot, Tony, to be honest. I'm tired carrying them on my back. It's time they learned to stand on their own feet.'

Lance moved furtively back into the picture.

'Look, this is all rather silly,' he said. 'Let's talk sensibly. As it happens, Conor, I was looking at your file this morning. Maybe it's time to have another look at your fee.'

He saw Conor about to interrupt, and carried on quickly.

'And, of course, there are other matters. As you rightly say, you've given us an enormous amount over the years and we should recognise that by, well, easing the load. Say, four weeks out. On full fee of course.'

'That's all you think it's about, Lance. You think, a few quid, a few perks, you can buy anybody. Well, you can't, not this time. I've given my life to this show and I want it back!'

He had rehearsed this line at home and was very

pleased with it. Lance retired to the window. Tony prepared to join the action, but Conor hadn't finished.

'Besides. Why should it end?'

'How do you suggest we keep it going?' said Tony, 'Without the main fucking character? Go on, tell us!'

'Any number of ways,' said Conor, tiredly. 'Off the top of my head, say, in this year's final episode, I die, in mysterious circumstances. They bury me. September, episode one, some detective inspector starts asking questions and they dig me up. State pathologist discovers traces of, I dunno... poisoned raspberry. Big murder investigation begins.'

He traced a headline in the air. '"Who killed Dermot Day?" Half a dozen suspects. Peter marries Lisa, so she can't testify against him. You've set that bit up already, remember?'

He looked hard at them and they looked back, unimpressed.

'Find the right actor for the inspector and you'll get a year out of that story.'

He walked to the door.

'Anyway, look, I've given you plenty of notice, I didn't have to do that.'

'We're very grateful,' said Lance.

And Conor left, leaving the door open.

* * *

168

Queenie had opened another bottle and they were sitting up in bed now, with full glasses.

'Could they not keep it goin' without you?'

'I suppose they could. Matter of fact, I gave them several suggestions. but I don't believe they will. They don't have a lot of imagination.'

'So what happens to them? Th'other actors.'

Conor sighed. 'Yeah, I feel really guilty about that. You see, I've wanted to get out before, but each time, I've been prevailed on to stay. They knew that if they could get me feeling guilty for the others, they could get to me. But this time, I'd made up my mind. And it's not just for my own sake, it's for them too.'

Queenie looked puzzled. 'Puttin' them out of work?'

'They're actors,' said Conor. 'It's not good for them, to go on in the same part, it makes them lazy. They have to get out there, show what they can do.'

He sipped his wine, shook his head.

'Besides, they're young, most of them. And they're known now, through the show. They won't have trouble getting work.'

'But why are you doin' it?'

He looked at her.

'I mean really. No spoofin'.'

'I've had enough, that's all. Fifteen years leading someone else's life. Make-believe life with make-believe people. Time I had a real life, with real people, people like you. I'd forgotten they existed.'

169

'Such a chancer,' she said, and put down her glass. 'Stop talkin' now and come here to me.'

He sighed, as if it was a penance, turned off his light and rolled over on her.

On her bedside table, under Queenie's lamp, he could see the picture of a little smiling Greek man, with one leg in the air.

* * *

Tony had switched on his goose-neck brushed chrome downlighter, which, when properly angled, made him look slim.

'It's finished, then?' said Lance.

'Of course it's finished,' said Tony. 'Only question is, how do we wrap it up?'

'You don't fancy "Who killed Dermot Day?"'

Tony shook his head. 'But I'd rather like it to be me,' he said.

'Well, we can't leave them all in bloody Wexford, growing old,' said Lance. 'So it comes down to the usual two choices. Death or emigration. Death is easier.'

'No,' said Tony. 'I'm against death.'

'Why?'

'Two reasons. One, I don't want the whole country mourning for the fucker. Two, he may yet change his mind.'

'So it's emigration?'

Tony nodded, and swivelled his leather-feel chair to face the opposite wall. The die was cast.

* * *

'Five minutes,' said the voice in Michael's earpiece, and he turned to camera.

'Earlier this evening,' he said, 'I was at Downhill Farm, County Wexford, watching the final scene of the final episode being shot. Of course, I've had to swear a fearful oath not to reveal what's in it.'

A loud 'Aah' from the audience denoted their disappointment, and Michael took his cue.

'Well, actually, we do have the last few moments on tape, and if we have time, we'll try to show you that before we go off air.'

They applauded approvingly.

'But I have to confess that, for me at least, it was rather moving. It seemed to me that, as the Day family said a last goodbye to Downhill Farm, the sadness wasn't just a performance. It was very real.'

He turned to Conor. 'Did you feel that?'

'Oh, it's… impossible to describe,' said Conor. 'It was like a dream, a journey into another place, another time. Leaving behind everything I knew. Every tree, every leaf.'

He shook his head and raised a hand to his brow, as if unable to go on. Eric looked at Liam and rolled a discreet eye upward. Michael looked respectful, as if intruding on

171

a private grief, despite a feeling that he had heard the speech before.

'But there was one odd thing about today wasn't there?'

Conor shot a curious look at him, not certain what was coming.

'They tell me,' Michael went on, 'and they were all quite amazed, that for the first time in the show's fifteen-year history, you were a half-hour late on set. Can you say why that was?'

Conor was disconcerted for a moment, but managed to get back into character.

'It was just such a difficult thing to face. The last time I would put on the battered moleskins, the old moth-eaten cap, and walk through the little half-door. Most heartbreaking of all, the last time I would meet all these dear friends.'

He spread his arms wide, to include everyone on stage. The theatre was hushed, as he went on.

'There's a little bistro close to where I live. I go there whenever I want to get away, be by myself. I dropped in there to have a drink. Stiffen my resolve, I suppose.'

* * *

It was late afternoon when he reached the café. The quiet time. As he opened the door quietly and went in, he heard the whistling and smiled. He stood a moment by the door, listening, wincing a little.

The tune, if you could call it that, was 'I get knocked down, but I get up again, Ain't never gonna keep me down, I get knocked down' … and on and on and on.

It was an odd choice for whistling, since there were only two notes. Maybe it was playing on a radio somewhere in the background and she was whistling along.

He tiptoed to the open door of the kitchen and peeped in, staying out of sight. Queenie, in cap and apron, stood by the worktop, her back to the door, preparing food and whistling. An open bottle of wine stood on the worktop, and beside it a glass, brimful. For a moment, maybe half a bar, she suspended the music, had a quick slurp of wine, then carried on. Under cover of the whistling, Conor slipped in and seized her waist. She screamed and dropped knives and skewers and bits of pork before he turned her around.

'Jesus, Conor, what are you doin' to me?' she said.

'Sorry.'

'I could've amputated meself.'

He stooped to help her pick up the fallen bits, then watched as she went back to work, cutting pieces of onion and red and green peppers, and placing them alongside rows of little cubes of pork. When he had called on her before, it had usually been at night, and there had been a kind of weariness about her, at the end of a long working day. It would disappear briefly when they were making love, but afterwards it would come back and she would want to sleep. Now there was no sign of it.

173

She sang suddenly, in a very small, clear voice. 'I get knocked down, but I get up again.' And stopped just as suddenly. 'Here get yourself a glass.'

'No, I can't. I'm going to work.'

'At this hour?'

'I'm on my way. The last time.'

She stopped work to look up at him. 'Ah, it's not!'

'I told you. Weeks ago.'

She remembered now.

'Yeah, you did, sure I've no head. But why's it so late? Isn't it usually the crack of dawn?'

'It's an evening scene. Then the wrap.'

'The wha'?'

'The final wrap. The party.'

She smiled. 'I suppose the drink'll flow. Drownin' your sorrows.'

He smiled back. 'Any excuse. Actually, I'm in no form for it.'

'Ah, go on with you. Sure, you'd drink it off a sore leg.'

'Not tonight. I'm going to slip away. I should make it back by ten, ten-thirty.'

She looked at him, uncertainly.

'That's why I called,' he said. 'I thought you might close early. We could have a late meal, then.'

She touched his hand, stopping him. 'No, Conor, not tonight.'

'Why not?'

'I can't. I mean, you never said.'

He looked surprised, upset.

'Well I kind of… thought you'd be here.'

She interrupted. 'It's your big night, you and your friends, from the show. You have to spend it together.'

He spoke quietly, shaking his head.

'There's only one person I want to spend it with.'

Queenie turned away and busied herself at her work, not looking up.

* * *

It had been a fine summer's afternoon at the location of Downhill Farm, where the cast and crew were making preparations for the final shoot. Riggers laid cables and stage hands loaded furniture into the truck. The cast stood about, in costume. A make-up girl went from one to another, doing what make-up girls do. Lance detached himself from a cameraman and joined Eric and Lance, who stood in the doorway of their cottage, looking at the sky.

'Where is our wandering boy?' said Eric.

'Oh, he'll turn up,' said Lance.

He looked at his watch. 'He's got a good half hour.'

'Not like him at all,' said Liam. 'He's usually prowling about before any of us. Preparing.'

'Talking to the trees,' said Eric.

'Sniffing the pigshit,' said Liam.

Sam, dressed and made up as the rosy-cheeked Lisa, came to join them. 'No sign of Bollocky?'

Lance shook his head.

'Did you try his mobile?'

'Never knew he had one,' said Lance.

'I have his number somewhere,' said Sam. 'I'll get it.'

She moved away to the house. Lance looked up at the sky, beginning to worry.

* * *

In the kitchen of the Café Vangelis, Queenie switched on the light and went back to her work, arranging the cubes of pork artistically on the skewer, separating one from another with the pieces of onion and red and green pepper. Conor watched her.

'What is it?' he asked.

'*Souvlaki.*'

'New one on me.'

'It's as common as dirt in Greece.'

'I never saw it on the menu.'

"Tisn't on it. It's a kind of special.'

She went on working. She knew there was no reason for feeling uneasy, but she did. And finally, as casually as she could, she said it.

'It's for Vangelis.'

He stared at her, not quite understanding. He had known there was something. A look he had not seen before.

'He's here,' she said.

Conor looked up and around, as if expecting to see him, a handkerchief in his hand, his leg in the air.

'Here in Dublin,' said Queenie. 'On a ship. Didn't I tell you he worked on the ships?'

Conor nodded. 'The bad penny.'

'Yeah,' said Queenie. 'Well, he's here. He's docked down the North Wall. Rose has gone to pick him up. She's real excited. Like, she was always fond of him.'

'Well, of course. He's her father.'

Conor was unsure where this was leading, how he should be reacting.

'He always brought her things. Little things.'

Conor nodded, approving. Good for Vangelis.

'He's been in poor health, you see. He has to give up th'old life, on the ships. He has to get treatment.'

All the time, as she talked, she went on working. The first kebab was done and she was threading the second.

'*Souvlaki's* his favourite,' she said.

Conor was more confused than ever. What did it mean? How should he deal with it?

A phone rang out. Queenie looked around. 'Must be yours,' she said.

He pulled it from his pocket, switched it off and put it back.

'You understand, Conor, don't you?' said Queenie. 'Sure, how could I turn him away?'

'Of course you couldn't,' he said quickly. 'Not to see him would be cruel. It wouldn't be in your nature.'

He felt relieved. She was sorry for him, that was it.

And Queenie was just as relieved that he seemed to understand and accept.

He pulled her close and kissed her. She allowed him, but did not respond. And in a moment, she drew away, back to the *souvlaki*.

'Are you not due at work?' she asked.

'They can wait,' he said. And to show how little he cared, he poured wine into a glass and drank it back. When he spoke, he was his old calm, confident self.

'When does his ship sail?' he asked.

'It turns around in three days.'

He nodded, and moved towards her again, but she drew back, seeing that he had misunderstood. And that she had to set him right.

'But he won't be going,' she said.

Conor stared at her.

'He's staying here, with me.'

10

Michael glanced at the clock, a little worried. Not about over-running. The show was not live, and this was what editors were paid for. What worried him was Conor, who seemed miles away. He was, after all, the star of the show, and seemed not to know where he was. Something was wrong.

'You're telling us,' he said, 'that you went for a drink?'

'Yes,' said Conor. 'Obviously, I stayed there too long. I suppose I couldn't face the fact that something so important, so dear to my heart, was ending.'

* * *

Conor stood staring at Queenie, unbelieving.

'You're taking him back?'

'Yes,' she whispered.

He shook his head, not understanding. 'You mustn't. You can't make that kind of sacrifice.'

'It's not a sacrifice,' she began, but he talked her down.

'I know what it can do to people. Giving up their lives to look after someone. You must know that, you've done it all your life.'

'Conor, listen to me, that's not the way it is.'

But Conor was not listening. 'I did the same, all those years. I know what it's like, putting family first, while your own life drains away.'

She was staring at him, shaking her head.

'But that wasn't you,' she said. 'Conor listen to me. That was the other fella… the one in the story. You keep doin' that, talkin' as if it was *you*.'

But he wasn't listening. He took her shoulders.

'It's time to think of your own happiness.'

'That's what I am thinkin' of. It's all I ever thought of.'

He was listening now and she lowered her voice.

'Do you not see, Conor? I love Vangelis.'

He looked at her blankly, as if he had not heard, then he shook his head.

'You love me,' he said.

'No!' She wriggled free of him. 'I've enjoyed being with you. It's not the same!'

He was still shaking his head, blocking out the idea.

'You're lying. Lying to yourself. You're sorry for him, you think you have to take him in, but you don't love him.'

She was angry now. 'Don't talk like that, Conor!'

'Like what?'

'Like an actor! I never loved you. I made love with you because I was lonely. There now.'

He was still shaking his head, not listening, carrying on a monologue, as if she wasn't there.

'I'm not giving you up, Queenie.'

'Ah, will you stop,' she said, trying to humour him. 'Haven't you given up plenty before this? The girls have told me.'

'That's true. Beautiful women. Anyone I wanted.'

'So why is it so...'

Again he talked her down. 'But I took you – a little, dried-up skivvy in a back kitchen.'

She drew in her breath. 'Well, I'm sorry if I spoiled the plot.'

He looked down at her.

'You know what I gave up. Left the show, walked away from everything.'

'You shouldn't have.'

'And you know why. It was all for you.'

'I never asked you to.'

'I told you.'

'Well, maybe you did, I don't remember, but if you did say it, I never thought you meant it, I thought it was just talk.'

He paused a moment, to catch his breath.

'This Vangelis. Your husband. The little sailor. Little feet. Little fat belly.'

'That's him.' She was angry now, wanting only to be

rid of him. 'But can I tell you somethin', Conor? When you and I were makin' love, I used to close me eyes and pretend it was Vangelis.'

She turned away from him.

'You can't do it,' he said. 'I won't let you.'

She spoke without turning round.

'Go on now, Conor. I don't want you here when he comes.'

'I won't let him have you,' he whispered.

She was finishing the third of the *souvlakis*. Concentrating, as if nothing was more important, she picked up the little cube of meat, centred it carefully and pushed the sharp point of the skewer through the soft flesh. It must be perfect for Vangelis.

Conor reached over her shoulder and took the last of the skewers. There was no other way. She would have to go.

He hesitated for a moment, then drew the skewer back and plunged it into her neck, below the lobe of her ear. The blood spurted out and she gave a little cry and tried to turn. He pulled it out, plunged it in again and pushed her to the floor, where she lay staring up, unbelieving, her blood spreading over the white tiles.

He looked at the blood on his hand, then held it under the tap and watched it wash away. For a moment he was twelve years old again, Lady Macbeth in the school play. From below, he heard a very small voice say his name, but he would not look down. He walked quickly from the kitchen. As the street door slammed, the phone rang in the café, but there was no-one to answer it.

* * *

The sun had reached the top of the poplars fringing the yard at Downhill Farm.

The cast and crew stood ready to record, among them a girl from wardrobe, standing by with Conor's costume, and someone from make-up, though they knew he preferred to do his own.

Lance would have been tearing his hair out, if he had had any.

'Where the fuck is he?' he said, not for the first time.

'You tried his flat?' said Luke, trying to help. Lance glared at him.

'His flat, his mobile, the caff around the corner, no replies, nothing.'

He looked up at the sky. 'We have about ten minutes' light left.'

'Don't panic old boy,' said Eric. 'He's always shown up.'

At that moment, a taxi drove fast into the yard and Conor jumped out.

No 'Sorry about that,' no explanation. Nothing.

'Somebody pay that,' he said, tearing off his coat and scarf. The PA ran to the taxi, opening her purse, and make-up and wardrobe hurried over. Lance was normally one to spread calm, but not now.

'Where in Christ's name have you been?' he started, but Conor cut him short.

'Save it, we don't have time.'

He had already pulled off his jacket and shirt and was pulling on the old denim. The girl from make-up dabbed at his face and neck as best she could.

'You realise the light's almost gone? You've put the whole shoot in danger.'

'Lance, you want this scene?' Conor was blazing. 'Then shut your fucking face!'

He pulled on the jacket, the old, check cap. The trembling wardrobe girl offered the trousers but he ignored them, and shoved the make-up girl aside.

'That's plenty – get lost now!'

And he turned on the other actors who had stood watching the performance.

'Why aren't you in position? Jesus!'

They scattered. Lance took over.

'All right, places everybody! No time for rehearsal, we're going for a take. Ten seconds.'

They had all hurried to their opening positions. Maire, Aisling, Lisa and Stephen in the Jeep, Dermot at the back of the truck, with Peter and Luke, Eric and Liam watching from the door of their cottage. Lance continued the count.

'Five… four… three… two… and… Action!'

184

EXT. FARMYARD. EVENING.

Outside the barn stands the truck. The Jeep is parked by the farmhouse door. Dermot is tying down the back gate of the Jeep, which is packed tight with cases, tea-chests, etc.

Outside the barn, Peter and Luke are doing similar jobs with the truck, which contains the heavier furniture, bolting the tailgates, checking the tyres.

Dermot is watched from the door of the house by Liam and Eric. There is a general air of sadness. Dermot tightens the last bolt.

LIAM

That'll do her.

Dermot turns and offers his hand.

DERMOT

Sorry it had to end this way, lads.

LIAM

(A toss of the head) Sure what harm? I was

thinkin' of takin' early retirement anyway.
The redundancy package.

Dermot grins and takes Eric's hand.

DERMOT

You'll look after him, Eric?

ERIC

(Unsmiling) Isn't it a pity they closed the
workhouse?

DERMOT

Who needs it? Your home's safe.

LIAM

Don't know about that. Once you're gone
they could knock the whole lot. Put up a
nightclub.

DERMOT

(Shakes his head) It's in the contract. Yours
for life.

ERIC

Jaze, now, Dermot. No man could have done
more.

* * *

On the kitchen floor of the Café Vangelis, Queenie lay still, her eyes closed. The skewer hung limply from her neck, in a little stream of blood, though the bleeding had stopped.

Outside, the street door opened and her eyes flickered. There were two voices, and she knew both. Her eyes went still again. Then the kitchen door opened and Rose and Vangelis came in. Rose saw her and screamed, and as Vangelis stood transfixed, she fell to her knees beside her mother. At the sound of the scream, Queenie opened her eyes and saw Rose looking down, wild-eyed.

'Mam!'

'Rose, is it yourself?' she whispered. 'Did you meet him? Where is he?'

Vangelis knelt now and took her hand. He looked just as he always had, a little thinner, a little greyer. Rose spoke through tears.

'What happened, Mam? Who did it to you?'

Queenie raised a hand to the skewer, as if to pull it out.

'No, Mam, leave it, it'll only start the bleedin' again.'

Queenie's eyes closed again.

'Mam!'

There was no response and Rose stood up.

'I'm ringin' th'ambulance,' she said, and hurried out to the café.

Vangelis stayed kneeling.

'Vasilissa,' he whispered. '*Agapi mou.*'

Rose's voice came through from outside.

'I need an ambulance... quickly please... it's really urgent.'

Vangelis leaned closer. *'Mi pethanis agapi mou.... don't die, Vasilissa...'*

She opened her eyes.

'Indeed'n I won't,' she whispered. 'I'll be all right now.'

The tears were springing from Vangelis's eyes and Queenie raised her hand and touched them.

'Don't now... I'm all right. Didn't I always tell you I had a hard neck?'

'Café Vangelis,' said Rose. 'Bridge Street, off Merchant's Quay. No, she's awake, but she's losin' blood. For God's sake hurry.'

Queenie turned her head a little and saw that something had fallen from the table and was spattered with blood.

'Ah look,' she said. 'Your *souvlaki's* ruined.'

* * *

'Tell me, Conor,' said Michael. 'And... er... try to be brief. How do you account for your popularity?'

'As you well know, Michael,' said Conor, 'it's the show that's popular.' He spread his arms wide to embrace everyone on stage. 'I'd be nothing without this lot.'

'So, tell me. If it's so popular – and it plainly is – why is it ending? Why are the Days leaving home?'

Conor leaned back, looking at the ceiling, as if marshalling his thoughts.

'Well, we were never too secure, right from the beginning. The fire was our first disaster, of course. We didn't have the barn insured, so we had to go into debt to build a new one. Then two years ago the floods – remember? Our entire crop lost. And in the middle of all that, there was Aisling's operation.'

In the second row, Aisling smiled self-consciously.

'Luke's drug bust,' said Michael.

'I was innocent!' shouted Luke.

The audience laughed, but Conor seemed not to notice. He was still in the past, calling it all back.

'We persuaded the bank to stake us for one more year. And it was all looking good, but then we had the late frost in May. Wiped us out.'

Something was not right. Among the cast there were uneasy glances. And Michael had the growing feeling that he was not getting through. He tried again.

'I suppose what I'm really asking…'

And again, Conor seemed not to hear.

'It wasn't something any of us wanted. After fifteen years living and working in that beautiful place. Loving it, too. I think we all loved it.'

Realising that somehow he had to stop this, Michael broke in.

'What you're telling me, Conor,' he said, 'is why *Dermot Day* had to leave Downhill Farm. But what I'm

189

asking you is why *Conor O'Hara* – and all these talented people – why you are all leaving our screens. Why now, at the height of your popularity? Why are you walking away?'

For a split second, Conor looked confused, like a driver who has dozed off at the lights and awakes to find they've turned to green and the whole world is sounding its horn.

By now, the audience were joining in Michael's question, shouting, 'Why?…'

'Go on,' said Michael. 'Tell them.'

Conor shrugged and smiled. It was the old Conor again. Measured, modest, in control.

'Well, I suppose it's good to stop when you're ahead. Leave them wanting more. Everything comes to an end. I've loved every minute of these last fifteen years. Every minute of every day, if you'll pardon the pun. But enough is enough. I'd just… hate us to outstay our welcome.'

Someone in the audience shouted, 'No!'

Another shouted, 'Stay!'

Dick sprang into action and began conducting a chant of 'Stay! Stay! Stay!'

'I think they want you to stay,' said Michael.

Conor started to speak, then stopped and shook his head. Overcome. No words.

Liam leaned over to Eric.

'Lovely artist,' he whispered.

Eric nodded, lost in admiration.

190

'I can't believe we've seen the last of Dermot Day,' said Michael.

Conor spoke quietly, but leaned towards the mike, to make sure he was heard.

'Well, you know what they say... Never say never.'

Quite unbidden, the audience broke into applause, during which the actors on stage looked at each other, their faces lighting up. For a moment, Dick forgot his duties and looked across at Eve. Lance and Tony exchanged a glance, which, as always with those two, said nothing. Eric and Liam smiled bleakly.

EXT. FARMYARD. EVENING.

Aisling, in tears, moves from Liam to Eric, kissing both.

AISLING

Oh Liam, Eric, what'll we do without you?

LISA

We'll write.

AISLING

And we'll come back and see you.

MAIRE

And bring you both a kilt.

Peter looks up at the sky.

PETER

Time we were gone, if we want the last of the light.

Luke and Peter move to the truck. Dermot opens the doors of the Jeep for the girls and climbs in himself.

LIAM

What way are ye going?

DERMOT

N11 to Dublin, straight to the North on the M1, then the ferry from Larne. It's a fine evening. Should be a good crossing.

He starts the engine, then turns to take a last look at the house. As the Jeep moves slowly off, the girls make little waves with their fingers and shape their lips into goodbyes.

*First the Jeep, then the truck, move
out of the yard.*

EXT. FARMYARD. EVENING.

*Another angle. From the road, as the
two vehicles come out. The final shot
of the family is as they pass the sign
that says 'Downhill Farm'.*

*The two vehicles go off down the road
and out of sight. The final shot is of
the house, as the last rays of the sun
dip below the Blackstairs Mountains.*

In the theatre, Dick allowed the final tableau to remain a
full five seconds before giving the signal for applause.
And though the final scene contained no great surprise,
they applauded long and loud. It was as if they too were
saying their goodbyes to Downhill Farm.

Michael made his way back across the stage and stood
before Conor, holding the red book before him.

'And with that,' he said, 'All that remains for me to say
to you, Conor O'Hara, to your alter ego, Dermot Day, and
indeed to all the Days of Downhill Farm… This…. Has
Been… Your Life.'

The applause renewed itself, louder than ever, as
Conor stood to take the book, and like the conductor of an

orchestra, signalled to all his colleagues to stand with him and take their bows. Together, and with the theme music of *The Days* playing loudly, they walked down to the footlights, smiling and waving to the standing audience, Conor in the middle, flanked by his two wives, Sam and Linda, the faithful retainers, Eric and Liam, and all the rest of the Days.

Backstage, Conor made his way down the narrow corridor to his dressing room.

As he went, his head as always down, people connected with the show, researchers, stage-hands, wardrobe, make-up, pressed back against the walls to let him pass, and called his name.

'Congratulations, Conor.'

'Great show, Conor.'

Then, reaching the door with the big gold star, he went inside and stopped in his tracks. Three dark-blue uniforms, peaked caps, one inspector, two guards, standing before his dressing table, making the little room more cramped than ever.

'Conor O'Hara?' said the inspector.

'Yes?'

He smiled, but the inspector was having none of it.

'I've had a complaint regarding an incident earlier this evening, as a result of which I'm arresting you on a charge of assault causing grievous bodily harm.'

'She's not dead, then?' said Conor, faintly, and one guard shot a glance at the other.

The inspector carried on as if no-one had spoken.

'You do not need to say anything, but anything you do say may be taken down in writing and used in evidence.'

The two guards stepped forward, one holding handcuffs. Conor backed away.

'Are they necessary?'

The inspector looked at the guard, who shrugged and put them away.

The other guard opened the door, holding it open for Conor to follow. Conor picked up his coat.

'Could I ask one favour?' he said.

They waited. 'May I walk ahead of you? Just a step.'

The guards looked at the inspector, who hesitated.

'Where can I run?'

The inspector nodded to the others and they stepped aside. Conor slipped easily into his lightweight cashmere and turned up the collar. Remembering the red book, he picked that up too and went out. The guards followed.

It was a warm night, and outside the theatre, many of the audience and some of the passers-by lingered to see the celebrities emerge. As Conor appeared, a cheer went up. People called his name – both his names – and popped flashlights. Conor waved in reply and the guards waited respectfully in the background. One of them indicated the unmarked car they were using, and Conor walked, smiling happily, towards it. He stood aside to allow the guard to open the doors, then turned again and gave a final wave before stepping into the back seat. The inspector sat in beside him, and with the two guards in front, the car moved slowly off. Conor had lowered his window, and the cheers followed the car, and the squad car coming behind it.

On the steps of the theatre, Eric and Liam stood watching.

'The ultimate accolade,' said Eric. 'A police escort.'

As the car increased speed and the sound of cheering died away, Conor wound up his window and turned to the inspector. A little smile, half-dazed, half-manic.

'Did you hear them?' he whispered.